"[illegible] hero."

Madison whispered the words as she stared at him, mesmerized. Then she cleared her throat. "You look exactly like my Black Jack, the way I see him, I mean. The eyes, the hair, the cleft in your chin... You're perfect."

"I know," he muttered.

"You move like him, you sound like him, you even dress like him."

Madison's eyes moved from his dusty cowboy boots over the lean length of his disreputable jeans, lingering on his worn fly. She felt her face flame just thinking about what was underneath.

She shifted her focus up to his black cotton shirt. Past his rolled-up sleeves, exposing strong, corded forearms, she saw his open collar, undone three buttons down to reveal the shadow of dark hair. He had a beautiful chest, muscular and broad. He really *was* perfect.

And whatever the indefinable quality that Madison had tried to brew into Black Jack Brogan—savvy, sizzle, all-out steam—this guy had it. Lots of it.

ABOUT THE AUTHOR

Julie Kistler owns a replica of the Maltese Falcon and routinely sends birthday cards to Fred Astaire. Her as-yet-unfulfilled ambitions include meeting Paul Newman, catching a home-run ball hit by Harold Baines of the Chicago White Sox and winning an Academy Award for anything. While working on those, Julie graduated Phi Beta Kappa from college, got a law degree, married a man she adores and dissolved her relationships with the legal profession on grounds of mutual boredom. She and her husband now live in Illinois, where they have produced one black cat with white paws and a newsletter about the sport of boccie ball.

Books by Julie Kistler

HARLEQUIN AMERICAN ROMANCE

158–THE VAN RENN LEGACY
207–CHRISTMAS IN JULY
236–WILDFLOWER
266–ALWAYS A BRIDESMAID
329–BEST WISHES
418–CHRISTMAS IN TOYLAND
429–FLANNERY'S RAINBOW
471–FINN'S ANGEL

JULIE KISTLER

BLACK JACK BROGAN

Harlequin Books

TORONTO • NEW YORK • LONDON
AMSTERDAM • PARIS • SYDNEY • HAMBURG
STOCKHOLM • ATHENS • TOKYO • MILAN
MADRID • WARSAW • BUDAPEST • AUCKLAND

Published May 1993

ISBN 0-373-16485-8

BLACK JACK BROGAN

Printed in U.S.A.

Chapter One

Half the world thought he was safely six feet under. But he wasn't. He wasn't planning on joining Saint Peter for a good long time. Not until he found the man who'd shot him and left him for dead, with only the coyotes and the Comanches for company. A grim smile crossed Black Jack's face.

And when he found his quarry, the battle would begin.

Black Jack Brogan, Book # 12
Jack in the Saddle Again

Black Jack Brogan was alive. Alive and well and knocking back tequila in Godforsaken, Texas.

It was impossible, of course. Dumbstruck in the doorway of the dusty cantina, Madison Talley stared at him, blinked, and stared again. But he was still there, big as life. Bigger than life.

Madison began to sweat and feel a little weak in the knees. Black Jack had always had that effect on her.

Gathering her wits, she sneaked to a nearby table, even ordering a shot of tequila herself. As well as clearing her head, she hoped it would make her blend in with the hard-drinking crowd in this dump of a saloon, giving her a chance to get a better look at the impostor. Because he had to be an impostor. She knew better than anyone that there was no Black Jack, except in her own fertile imagination.

"Black Jack Brogan is fiction," Madison whispered, trying to convince herself her eyes had deceived her. "I made him up myself."

Too bad Mr. Big-as-Life didn't look a thing like fiction. In fact, he looked like the answer to a grown woman's dreams. Ditching that thought, she gulped the tequila down, choking and wheezing when it hit her throat like a nuclear blast.

Whew. She tried not to notice the steam coming out of her ears as she put a hand over her mouth to muffle the coughs. Well, that certainly cleaned out the old sprockets, didn't it? Now, instead of merely wilting in the oppressive heat, she was being scorched from the inside out. But the liquid fire of the tequila didn't do a thing to solve the problem of Black Jack Brogan brought to life. In fact, as it sent flames shooting into her empty stomach and through her veins, her vision grew a little fuzzier and Black Jack looked even better.

"Impossible," she muttered, eyeing him darkly as he slapped his cards facedown on the small scarred table and then blew out a cloud of smoke from a foul-looking cigar. "Utterly and completely impossible."

She'd been very canny when she created him, purposely starting with the traits she thought would sell to a publisher. At the time she'd needed work desperately, and she'd hoped she could put together a really dynamite character as a hook to sell a whole series. But Black Jack didn't like being a mere marketing ploy.

Before she knew it, he'd swept her away. As she wrote her books, Jack pushed her and aggravated her and demanded her absolute best. Forgetting about what was salable and what wasn't, Madison wrote from her gut. Black Jack wouldn't have it any other way.

She hadn't intended it, but he ended up the sum and substance of her darkest and dreamiest fantasies. Every hair on his head, every angle of bone, every bulge of muscle—she crafted them to be absolutely, gut-wrenchingly perfect. He was, after all, the hero of all seventeen of her bestselling Western-romance-adventure novels, and she'd had to make him pretty darned spectacular.

Okay, so she was suffering from a mammoth case of writer's block on number eighteen, but that was hardly Black Jack's fault. No, he was wonderful. Stubborn, arrogant, sexy as hell—he was a bad boy, and he was wonderful.

She'd written him as a spy during the Civil War in *Union Jack,* gambling and gunfighting in Dodge City in *Jack's Wild,* even seducing one of Queen Victoria's less virtuous daughters to safeguard state secrets in her own personal favorite, *Jack Be Nimble, Jack Be*

Quick. If it was outside the law, financially rewarding, and very, very dangerous, then the Black Jack of her imagination was undoubtedly involved up to his gorgeous eyeballs.

So what the heck was he doing, sprawled at a dusty table in a scummy cantina, chomping a noxious cigar, hustling a motley crew of smelly men in a disreputable poker game? Her hero would never stoop so low. This joint was too low rent for Black Jack Brogan.

Her heart pounded harder and her knees got wobblier the nearer she edged, but Madison forced herself even closer. She wished she had a fake mustache or a cowboy hat to hide behind. But disguised or not she had to see him up close, to get a feel for what this guy was doing and why he looked so much like her very own Black Jack.

Biding her time, she fingered her right earring, a recycled bottle cap with tiny toy silverware hanging from it. Her earrings were her fashion statement, and just touching one of them seemed to calm her.

Carefully, quietly, she eased into a chair right next to his table, choosing one turned away from him for better camouflage. Meanwhile, he seemed to be completely focused on his poker game, and he paid no attention as she sank down in the chair, inching her head around, until she could get a full view without obviously staring.

It was uncanny.

"Impossible," she whispered again. From his scuffed boots to the black shadow of his three-day beard, this was the Jack she knew. This look-alike, this impostor, had the same piercing gray eyes under slanting black brows, the same narrow, sexy lips, the rakish nose, even the small cleft in his chin. He even had that reach-out-and-whip-you sexual pull she'd thought was a myth when she gave it to Black Jack.

She didn't know what to do. It was one thing to deal with her hero on paper; it was quite another to see him in the living, breathing, pulsating flesh. She felt like fainting. She felt like tossing back another shot of tequila.

Mostly, she felt like running back to her motel and changing her clothes. *Vanity, thy name is Madison,* she thought grimly. It was the dopiest thing she'd ever considered, but for some reason she was miserable to think Black Jack would see her for the first time wearing grubby shorts and a tank top.

Madison shivered. Black Jack, real. It was enough to make her melt into a puddle of anxiety. Trying not to get any unwelcome notice from the poker players, she attempted to order another shot of tequila, but the scuzzy waitress had draped herself and her dyed blond hair all over the largest of the poker players, one with a big blue "Mom" tattoo on his forearm.

They were a real pair of cuties, him with his bulging muscles bursting out of a denim vest and her stuffed into a leather miniskirt and a glow-in-the-dark orange halter top that emphasized the massive dimensions of her bosom. Apparently, the waitress was too occupied ogling the blue tattoo to be bothered to serve customers at the moment. So Madison was going to have to be content to stay parched and sticky, without even a glass of water to tide her over.

But she refused to budge, even to go find cooler, wetter surroundings. No, it was too interesting where she was. As Madison kept her furtive watch, she surmised that Jack was winning; he had the biggest pile of money in front of him, and he continued to add to it as the cards were dealt and dealt again. She also could tell that the other louts at his table were getting restless and cranky, while her hero remained silent.

Trouble, she thought. Either Jack was cheating or he was amazingly lucky. She couldn't help a small smile of triumph. Of course he was lucky. Hadn't she written him that way herself?

But the rumbles from the other table didn't sound good and Madison felt her own anxiety level rise. Wiping moisture from her brow with the back of one hand, she wished it weren't so darned hot, wished she hadn't sat so close to that table full of teeming manhood.

Tattooed and leather-clad, the other three men smelled to high heaven, like sweat and dirt, like a couple hundred miles of bad road. But their odor and their macho posturing weren't what she found so overpowering. As she sat there, feeling a trickle of perspiration slide down between her breasts, drowning in heat, breathing dust and tequila fumes, she tried hard not to notice.

But there was no avoiding it. There was some sort of energy, a feeling of repressed anger, emanating from Jack himself, and the vibrations crept out and wound around her, willing her to come closer, to soothe his fevered brow. It was only with the severest infliction of self-control that she held her ground, faced away from Black Jack.

The funny thing was, she knew without any doubt that he was as much of a stranger here as she was. The others might be regulars, but not him. The way he held himself, the way the motorcycle thugs acted toward him—even the way the brassy waitress kept sending him curious glances. It added up to a stranger, and Madison was glad. In her heart, she didn't want him to be the sort of person who hung out in places like this, even if he was an impostor.

Meanwhile, the insults and the muttering continued to grow. Finally one of the men pushed away, hurling his cards to the table as he rose with an angry roar.

"You're one damn lucky son of a bitch," he growled. "Cleaned me out. I been trying to catch you cheating and I can't see a damn thing. Lucky SOB."

With a string of oaths Madison had never heard before and never hoped to hear again, the angry gambler shoved his chair over and clomped out the door, briefly letting a triangle of hot Texas sun shine into the dark room. Madison squinted in the blaze of light, but her attention was still riveted to the scene behind her.

As the room fell silent, all she could hear was the sound of her own breathing. But then paper rustled as Jack fed money into the pile in the center of the table, raising the bet.

"Are you in or out?" he asked softly.

Her heart lodged in her throat. Even his voice was right on target. It was that perfect mix of dark and light, of silk wrapped around cold steel. Her fantasy man was coming true. She didn't know whether to be excited and thrilled—or just plain petrified.

"You got all my cash," the brute with the waitress on his lap said in a squeaky little voice that wrecked his image. "I ain't got nothin' else to put in."

"You'll have to decide if you're paying up or pulling out."

"How 'bout this?" As Madison watched, the squeaky ox made a fist and shoved it inches from Jack's face. "My ring," he said, grinning, and Madison let out a small sigh of relief. At least he wasn't planning to rearrange Jack's perfectly carved features right in front of her.

"I'm not interested in jewelry," Jack said quietly.

"So what do you want?"

There was a pause, as everyone in the bar seemed to lean in closer to hear the answer. "Her," Jack said, easing back in his chair, flicking his gaze over the curves barely contained by the neon orange halter top.

Her? The waitress? Madison just about jumped up and throttled him. What could Black Jack possibly want with that disgusting sleazeball of a waitress? Okay, so she had breasts to spare, and she was perfectly willing to share them with anyone who cared to take a gander. But Jack had much higher standards than *that*.

She glowered at him. "Swine," she mumbled under her breath.

"Fine," returned the squeaky man, dumping the woman unceremoniously off his lap. "I call."

Madison could no longer contain her interest and she stared openly as Jack pulled up a chair for the waitress and then slowly laid down his cards. He had three twos. Three twos? That was all? She remembered researching poker when she'd written *One-Eyed Jack,* the riverboat-gambler book, but she still couldn't recall what counted for what. Nonetheless, she didn't think three twos was very impressive, and she smiled with satisfaction, glad that Jack was undoubtedly going to lose his money and his chance at a romp with Miss Halter Top.

She peered over Jack's shoulder as Squeaky slapped down his own cards. A pair of kings and a pair of queens. A gasp greeted the cards.

Madison assumed that meant Squeaky had won. His kings and queens certainly looked good to her. And if the big oaf had clobbered Jack, it was exactly what he deserved. But Jack just smiled, offering a slow, lazy grin that lifted one side of his mouth.

"Looks like I'm taking home the lady," he said calmly. And then he leaned over and began to gather in the pile of cash.

"Lady, my foot," Madison muttered. "Lady of the evening, maybe." But she had to keep it down, or she'd risk Jack hearing her, and then actually looking at her, and that wouldn't do at all. Ha. As if he'd have time to look at her with that cheap blonde in the way.

Meanwhile, she felt terribly cheated. How could three stinky little twos beat all those lovely face cards?

Unfortunately, nobody else seemed to think it was odd, and nobody moved to stop Jack from getting cozy with Miss Halter Top, after he'd safely collected the money.

As Jack whispered and smiled at her, the brassy waitress giggled, draping herself and her ample bosom over his arm and into his lap. The room full of riff-raff stood rapt with anticipation. How would the man with the blue tattoo respond? Was there going to be a knock-down-drag-out fight, right there in the cantina? The bartender quietly pulled a shotgun out from under the bar and held it at the ready.

Madison held her breath. For the first time, she began to understand exactly what sort of hole she'd wandered into and how dangerously out of place she was.

Squeaky sat there, beetle-browed, glaring at Jack, while Jack took a long drag on his cigar. He didn't waver under the scrutiny, keeping his own gaze steely and steady, and he didn't take his hands off the blonde, either. Tension hung in the air between Jack and the man with the blue tattoo. Finally, the big brute shoved himself away from the table and skulked over to the bar.

A hiss of disappointment slithered through the onlookers. The controversy had evaporated without so much as a punch being thrown. Clearly, they'd all hoped for some blood and broken bones.

"Hit me," Squeaky ordered in his whiny little voice. He hunched at the bar, throwing tequila back like water, shot after shot.

Madison swallowed, relieved beyond belief that no blows had been thrown, no altercation had broken out. But her relief was short-lived as she glanced around the bar. Had those thugs been eyeing her all along? Had she been too wrapped up in Jack to notice? She shuddered. The last thing she needed was to attract any kind of attention from this bar full of Neanderthals.

But still she refused to leave. Stubbornly, she clung to the notion that if she ignored all the stares and crude comments, they would simply go away. But she couldn't leave until she figured out what Jack was up to. After all, he couldn't possibly be interested in that horrid waitress, not in the way it seemed. No, he must have some other, more mysterious motive for wanting to win her in the poker game.

"What would he want with her?" Madison mused, watching him more openly now. Everybody else was gawking; why shouldn't she? Besides, it kept her mind off the fact that at least three of the motorcycle guys were giving her the once-over. "What would a man like Jack need from a sleaze like her?" she asked under her breath.

Only a master plotter like Madison Talley could figure this one out. She'd written Black Jack into trickier corners than this, of course, and she always had him romancing some woman or other, sometimes because she gave him a worthy romantic interest, but more often to pry out secrets to further the plot.

"Information," she said out loud. "Of course."

That drew a few glances, and she shut up quickly. Okay, so he was on to the blonde for information, to get the scoop on whatever undercover operation he was running. Madison smiled, proud of herself. Yes, it all fit nicely. Black Jack Brogan was conducting business as usual, consorting with unsavory characters not because he wanted to, but because he had to.

Whew. What a relief to know her hero didn't really like that hideous, positively vulgar woman. Undoubtedly, he would chat with his quarry for a few moments, until he heard what he wanted, and then he'd mosey out of there alone. She had no sooner convinced herself of that fact than she saw Jack lean in much closer, tighten his embrace, and whisper something that elicited wiggling and preening from the waitress.

Okay, so he was doing a good job, that was all. But then Miss Halter Top stood up, yanking her miniskirt down enough to barely cover her derriere. She fluffed her hair in a bad imitation of Marilyn Monroe, manufacturing a throaty voice to call out to the bartender, "I'm leavin' for the night, Mo."

"You're gone more'n you're here, Kandy," he growled, shaking his head.

"Gimme a break, Mo. I got me a live one." She inclined her thumb at Jack, and Madison felt like tossing her cookies right then and there. A "live one" indeed.

Relenting, the bartender said gruffly, "Get outta here."

"See ya," the girl returned saucily, dancing past the bar arm in arm with Jack.

Predictably, he said nothing. He didn't have to. His body language spoke volumes, warning off anybody who might step in between him and his newfound paramour. As if anybody would.

So there they were, waltzing out into the sunlight together, evidencing every intention of going somewhere and... Well, it was too disgusting to think about.

At that moment, Madison made up her mind. She didn't know exactly why, but she knew what she had to do. She was going to follow him, and she was going to make sure he didn't risk life and limb consorting with that piece of no-class trash.

And she certainly wasn't going to tarry one extra second in the scary saloon, rife with loathsome people, not after Jack left and took his protection with him. Okay, so he hadn't offered his protection, and in fact, had made no indication that he even noticed her existence. But she felt sure he would've protected her if the necessity had arisen.

He was, after all, the spitting image of Black Jack Brogan, and Jack always rescued damsels in distress. Madison raised her chin. She'd written him as a gentleman, hadn't she? Well, not exactly a *gentleman,* but close enough.

As soon as Jack and the floozy cleared the door, Madison was out of her seat and headed after them. She paid no attention to the catcalls from the other patrons, gritting her teeth and ignoring the hands that tried to grope her on her path between the tables. If she got out of there alive, she was going to count herself lucky. Finally, blessedly, she made it to the door, pushing the heavy thing open and blinding herself in the blaze of late-afternoon sunshine.

The dusty little town of Godforsaken had taken on a burnished orange glow as the sun beat down, still high in the sky. If anything, it was hotter than when she'd ducked into the cantina, and she wouldn't have believed that was possible.

Clearly, July in Godforsaken was not to be taken lightly.

Wishing she had one of those bandannas from the cowboy movies to mop the back of her neck, Madison feathered her spiky bangs through her fingers, trying to get more air on her face. Too bad there wasn't any air. It was just plain hot. And just plain unbearable.

The idea of the pool back at her motel began to seem as tempting as a mirage in the desert. But still her resolve remained firm. She was not going to let this Black Jack impostor out of her sight. So she continued trailing along behind him, stopping here and there to hide behind handy corners and doors so she wouldn't get spotted. All the while, she kept a vigilant eye on Jack and where he was headed.

He and Kandy were about a block ahead of her, scuffling dust with their feet as they turned down an alley. Madison followed carefully, poking her head around the corner before assuring herself they weren't looking her way. And then she, too, sneaked down the narrow path between the town drugstore and an out-of-business souvenir shop.

Small wonder it was out of business, she thought. Why in the world would anyone want souvenirs of a dump like Godforsaken? It wasn't as if there were any tourists. Okay, so she was a tourist and she was staying in Godforsaken. But that was a mistake, a screw-up back at the travel agency. She had intended to spend her vacation on an island somewhere, with sand and surf and lots of other tourists. Where there was something better to do than shadow a man who couldn't possibly be what he seemed.

Ahead of her, Kandy began singing some loud, lewd song, much more suitable to drunken sailors carousing in the wee hours of morning than Black Jack Brogan in the full light of day. Jack didn't sing along; he just kept directing her to walk on, practically pushing her down the street, while she pretended to be coy and cutesy. As if anyone in that sort of outfit had the slightest chance of seeming hard to get.

Watching the two of them, any onlooker would have concluded that Jack was hot to trot, that he couldn't wait to get the woman into bed. Madison, however, refused to believe it.

But what was she going to do if it were true? Did she really have enough guts to interrupt him on some pretext, just to keep him out of those inappropriate arms?

"I could always start a fire," she said hopefully. It would be a very satisfying feeling to burn him to the ground if he really did do something nasty with that woman.

But how was Madison going to know *what* he was doing? She could hardly spy on him that thoroughly, even if she wanted to, which she didn't. She felt her face flush just thinking about it. In this heat, she didn't need any more warmth in her face, but she had it, anyway, as she imagined the disgusting scene she might be about to witness.

Jack and the blonde had wandered down an even seamier street, stopping on a patch of scrubby grass out in front of a tumbledown house. Kandy threw her arms around him, giggling and clinging and motioning toward the small house.

So whose house was it? Hers? Or his? Or did it really matter? Madison bided her time behind a spindly tree half a block away, trying to decide what she was going to do when the gruesome twosome did the inevitable and went inside.

"Face it," she whispered. "You're going to walk back the way you came until you find someone who can tell you how to get back to that damn motel. And then you're going to sit by the pool and forget you ever saw this joker, who does not resemble Black Jack in the least."

But her gaze found him again, lounging in that scruffy yard, and she lingered there, drinking him in. Even paired with a tart, he was gorgeous. It was in the way he stood, all lean and rangy, deceptively lazy, but coiled and ready for God knew what. It was in the way his hair fell soft and dark across his forehead, begging to be brushed back. It was in the clean line of his jaw, the hint of softness in his lower lip, the unforgiving slant of his black brows.

"Face it," she said slowly. "He's Jack."

Nobody else had ever hit her right where it hurt. Nobody but Jack. In her heart of hearts, she had already accepted that this was him. Impossible, but true.

Wearily, Madison rubbed her hand over the back of her neck. Her hair was cut sinfully short, the coolest possible style in this abominable weather, but it was still soaked through with sweat and heat. Was she melting because it was a hundred degrees, or because she'd found the man of her fantasies?

"What am I going to do when they go inside?" she murmured.

But she didn't have to find an answer to that terrible question. As she watched, Jack disengaged himself from the girl's clinging embrace, ushered her up to the front door and forcefully closed the door behind her.

"She went in. And he didn't," Madison whispered in disbelief. Of course, it was what she'd been telling herself all along, but still... What a surprise to have it come true.

She had to rouse herself to keep tailing him; she almost lost him as he set off in the other direction down the street. He was moving more quickly without the blonde to slow him down, and Madison had to pick up her pace, too. But there he was, disappearing around the next corner, and she hopped to it, finding a store of energy she didn't know she had left.

She shadowed him for another two blocks before he took a sharp right, angling into what looked like a skinny alley or maybe a driveway, running between a dirty adobe grocery store and the back of an equally grubby gas station.

Where was he? She could've sworn he'd ducked in there, but when she peered down the alley, it looked empty. The narrow path between the buildings was a curious mix of shadows and sun and she had to squint to see at all, but she still couldn't make him out down there.

Cautiously, she inched into the dusty passage, sure she'd pick up his trail again on the other side. There was something funny about this innocent-looking alley, however, something that was giving her the willies, sending a shiver of alarm up her spine. She took the first few steps slowly, feeling along in front of her where the shadows obscured her view. The crouched, paranoid mode of travel made her feel silly, and she straightened, lifting her chin and proceeding like a brave, competent adult ought to.

And then someone grabbed her.

Before she had a chance to scream or anything else that might have been useful, she was spun around and slammed into a wall of adobe, her hands splayed on either side of her head.

Her back to the wall, she found herself staring up into the stormy eyes of Black Jack Brogan, in the flesh. The very real, very warm flesh. Pressed up against her. Very, very closely.

Madison tried to remember to breathe. But when he moved against her, getting a better grip, the feel of that strong, lean body knocked the wind right out of her.

"Who the hell are you and why are you following me?" he growled.

Chapter Two

He'd been in worse scrapes than this, but he'd never faced a meaner woman. Lola was as loco as a drunk coyote howling at the moon. She'd drugged him and tied him up and now she was standing there, inches away, taunting him.

"I always get what I want, Black Jack," she whispered from between those perfect ruby lips, and then she pulled out a knife.

Slowly, almost sweetly, she slid the wicked blade from the top to the bottom of his fly, popping buttons and slicing cloth, until the fabric hung open like a hungry mouth on a baby bird. She'd made her point.

"Are you going to give me what I want, Black Jack?"

He glanced down at his pants and then up at Lola's luscious curves. "I think that can be arranged."

"I thought so." She smiled. "I always get what I want."

Black Jack Brogan, Book # 17
Between a Jack and a Hard Place

Damn the woman, anyway.

He tightened his grip on her wrists, leaning in with a menacing glare. He was fully prepared to hold her against the wall until doomsday, or until she came clean, whichever was first.

She had already caused him no end of trouble. By peering over his shoulder and trying to eavesdrop, she'd almost distracted him enough to blow the poker game. Then she'd spied on him from behind a tree that wasn't big enough to hide a kid, definitely screwing up his chances with Kandy. Now here she was, caught dead to rights, and she didn't even seem worried.

She was a funny little thing, slender and lithe, with short-cropped black hair and pale, soft skin. Her dark green eyes were alight with excitement, and her lips were curved into a wide smile. It was a Dennis the Menace grin, chock-full of mischief, and he didn't find it endearing.

Smiling! What right did she have to be smiling? She should be scared out of her interfering little knickers. He could bluff his way out of a bar full of cranky bikers with one fierce stare, and yet he couldn't manage to throw a good case of panic into this skinny, irresponsible female who didn't have the sense to go in out of the sun.

He narrowed his gaze. Maybe that was the problem. Maybe she wasn't firing on all cylinders.

"Who are you?" he repeated, more slowly and meaningfully this time. "Why were you following me, and doing such a lousy job of it?"

"Lousy job?"

She bristled, losing the smile, wiggling under his hands, but he didn't let go. The way she was moving, she was getting herself all tangled up against him, her bare knee brushing his thigh, her breast just grazing the inside of his arm. God, it felt good.

Under his fingers, he could feel her pulse quicken and race, matching his own skyrocketing heartbeat. He tried to ignore it, but her little maneuvers were far more erotic than anything Kandy had tried, even if Kandy'd had a lot more practice.

The way this nuisance of a woman was making his body leap to attention, he began to wonder if maybe he shouldn't have tried to ditch her instead of confronting her. If the first two minutes he'd spent next to her were any indication, this was one troublesome female.

He edged off a step, just enough to keep her knee from rubbing his thigh, but he could still feel the heat emanating from her, could still see the thin trickle of perspiration sliding past the hollow of her throat, disappearing into her skimpy shirt right between her softly curving breasts. From his angle, he knew all he'd have to do was lean forward another inch or two, and he could taste the salty drop with his tongue, tracing its path all the way down. And then he'd peel off that negligible tank top and taste the rest of her.

Damn. He shut his eyes. He was much too close and much too hot.

Luckily, she seemed too riled up to notice the fire alarms. "There was nothing wrong with the way I followed you,'' she insisted, still struggling against his grip. ''I caught you, didn't I?''

''I caught *you,*'' he reminded her. ''Because you stuck out like a four-hundred-pound gorilla at a debutante ball.''

''I did not!''

''Listen, lady, you're at my mercy at the moment, and I'm not feeling any too merciful. So you better cut the comedy and tell me who the hell you are.'' He paused, skewering her with his steeliest gaze. ''Now.''

''I'm, uh, Madison Talley,'' she said quickly, sinking down a little under the force of his glare. ''You know, Black Jack Brogan.''

He lifted an eyebrow, not giving an inch. ''Am I supposed to know what that means?''

''Black Jack Brogan,'' she said patiently. ''You.''

''Me?''

''Exactly.''

''Exactly what?''

''Exactly you.''

She seemed to think that made perfect sense, even if he was at a loss to understand. Abruptly, he let go of her wrists, and she slid down off her tiptoes. But he kept one hand on the wall on each side of her, trapping her in the circle of his arms.

She smelled like flowers. In hundred-degree weather, fresh out of a smoky, sleazy bar and a blistering march around a blazing-hot town, she had the nerve to smell like flowers. He muttered an oath, averting his head so he didn't have to inhale her fragrance with every breath.

Angry with her, but mostly at himself, he growled, "Explain yourself. Quickly. I'm running right out of patience here."

She smiled again, with enough sparkle to put toothpaste ads out of business. "You know, you are so much like Black Jack, it's downright spooky. He cornered this Mata Hari type in *Between a Jack and a Hard Place,* and his dialogue sounded exactly like yours does right now. Of course, I'm hardly Mata Hari, but still, it's amazing how much you sound like him."

"*Between a Jack and a Hard Place?* Mata Hari? What the hell are you talking about?"

"Well, of course you wouldn't have heard of that one. It's my latest, and it isn't out yet. Not till Christmas."

"Your latest what?"

"Book," she explained, a little testy this time.

"Book?"

"I told you my name. Didn't you hear me?"

"I heard you. Are you saying you write books?"

"Of course I write books." Her eyes widened with dismay. "You mean you heard my name, but you didn't recognize it? Is this a joke?"

"I never joke. Am I supposed to recognize it?"

"Of course." Acting more than a little miffed, she said plainly, "I'm *Madison Talley.* I've been on the *New York Times* bestseller list twelve times, for goodness' sake! Where have you been?"

Clearly, she expected him to be impressed and deferential when he realized he'd accosted a famous author. Even if she was telling the truth, he wasn't impressed.

"Madison, huh?" he asked lazily. "What do they call you for short—Mad? Maybe Mad Dog?"

"Very funny."

"I've been captured by a woman named Mad." He shook his head. "Even I don't believe it."

"It's very strange that you've never heard of me," she said stiffly. "Where do you live, Mars?"

"I don't keep up with popular culture."

"Does that mean you don't read books?"

"That's what it means," he said coolly.

"What about television? Do you watch TV?"

"Nope. There aren't usually any in the places I find myself."

Madison frowned. "I didn't think there was anywhere without television in this day and age. Where do you live?"

"Oh, here and there."

His tone was casual, but he gave her a more careful appraisal. Was her interest as innocent as it seemed? Or was there something a little darker behind her questions? If she was a plant, the agency was certainly dipping into bizarre waters these days.

No, he couldn't believe Little Miss Mad had ulterior motives. Strange as it seemed, he actually found himself swallowing her story. Of course, that didn't explain what she was doing shadowing him, but at least it was a start.

"I can't believe you've never heard of me," she muttered, clearly stewing about it.

He had to catch himself before he smiled and ruined his Tough Guy image. She was really peeved, and he was enjoying it.

"Are you going to tell me why you were following me?" he demanded. He set his jaw so he wouldn't laugh. "Or am I going to have to get rough with you?"

"Don't be silly. Black Jack would never get rough with a woman." She chewed her lip for a second or two. "Of course, there was that time in *Jack in the Saddle Again* when he slugged that horrid woman who ran the brothel, but that was only after she hit him over the head with a spittoon. I mean, anyone would take umbrage at that, don't you think?"

Uh-oh. She was off in never-never land again. He couldn't remember ever being more surprised and confused by a woman. "What the hell are you talking about?"

But she wasn't listening. "And then there was Lola in *Between a Jack and a Hard Place.* He was pretty rough with her, but my goodness, she cut his pants off with a knife! He had to subdue her or she would've eaten him alive." She shook her head sadly. "Lola was one crazy cookie, let me tell you."

"Mad," he said gently. "Please. What are you talking about?"

"Jack." Surprised, she looked up, right into his eyes. "Black Jack Brogan. I told you that."

"But *why?* Why are you telling me this stuff? Why did you try to tail me?" He bent in closer, suppressing the urge to shut her up by covering her mouth with his for a good, long time.

"Well, I..."

"You do have a reason, don't you? Somewhere in that brain of yours?" He sighed. "You're not on a three-day pass from some kind of mental institution, are you?"

"Of course not. And yes, of course, I had my reasons for following you." She frowned at him. "I told you, I'm Madison Talley. If you had even the slightest connection to the real world, you would've heard of me, because as I told you—"

"Yeah, yeah, you're famous. Get to the point," he commanded.

"The point is, there's a perfectly reasonable explanation for all of this, and I'd be happy to share it with you."

"So share."

She paused, and he knew he wasn't going to like what came next. "Well, not here. I mean, I promise I can clear this all up," she tried, batting at him with those big green eyes. "Really. But don't you have a home base or anything?"

"A home?" His tone was more suspicious than he'd intended. "Why?"

"I thought maybe if you could, um, move your arms and sort of let me out of this..."

She set her hands on his arms, testing the bonds on either side of her. The feel of those soft little fingers pushing at him was enough to make him grit his teeth, but he didn't give in or let her go.

Nonplussed, she lifted her chin and met his gaze. "I thought if we weren't quite so constrained," she said primly, "it might be more conducive to a civilized conversation. So do you have someplace to go or not?"

Unlike Madison, he was able to give answers straight up, no frills. "I have a motel room. It's a dive."

"Okay then. Let's go."

He lifted an eyebrow. "You want me to take you back to my place?"

"Well, in a word, yes."

"Why, Mad, I didn't think you were that kind of girl."

She blinked. "What kind of girl?"

"Bored, lonely, on the prowl. Looking for some action."

"What?" she asked, gasping.

"Hot to go back to my place, huh? That would explain a thing or two, I guess." He gave her a leisurely look up and down. "You scope out the bar and there's not much to choose from, so I win the Mad sweepstakes, right?"

"Of course not." She swiped at the moisture on her forehead. "Well, actually, yes, but not in the way you're implying. I mean, there was no contest. I did see you and think to myself, I have to know what he's doing, but not like I was hot—well, I was hot, but not *that* kind of hot—"

He shrugged, ignoring her protests. She was getting all hyped up and bothered, and he was enjoying having the advantage in this conversation for once. "Yeah, it all fits," he continued coolly. "You tried to telegraph some interest during the poker game, hanging over my shoulder, breathing in my ear—"

"I never breathed anywhere near your ear!"

"But I wasn't buying, so then you decided to follow along and throw a wrench into my romantic rendezvous with Kandy—"

"Romantic rendezvous? More like sleeping with dogs and getting up with fleas, if you ask me."

"Jealous, huh? Well, you got rid of the competition, so you're top dog now. You've got me all alone, with plenty of opportunity to pitch this 'back to my place' shot. Sure, I get it." He winked suggestively. "Let's go, Mad. I can hardly wait to see what tricks you're into."

She blushed a very becoming shade of rose pink. "I'm not into any tricks. And I wasn't proposing *that* sort of... activity. I just wanted to talk to you."

"Yeah, right."

"It's true!"

"Why waste time on talk?"

"You're the one who keeps demanding answers." She crossed her arms over her chest, blocking his view of that enticing little rivulet of sweat. "By suggesting we go back to your place, I was only trying to offer the answers you so desperately crave, in a more private setting."

He gave her a half smile. "Private. I like that."

"Just stop it," she returned. "Do you want to hear me out or not?"

He shook his head. "Don't tell me. You want to chat about this Jack guy, and I'm supposed to sit there and patiently listen, is that the idea?"

She brightened. "Yes, exactly."

"And what do I get out of it?"

"Well, you get to know why I've been following you. Isn't that what you wanted?"

"Lucky me," he said grimly.

He needed his head examined. But he grabbed her hand and abruptly wheeled, towing her after him out of the alley.

"I don't suppose you'd let me go back to my hotel and change my clothes first," she ventured.

Without pausing to answer, he strode down the dusty streets of Godforsaken, back in the direction of his own motel. If that's where she wanted to go and if she'd give him some peace if he took her there, then by all means he was taking her there.

"No, I didn't think so," she murmured behind him.

He didn't have a clue what she was talking about, but that was nothing new. All he was going to do was deal with this Mad-woman and her imaginary friends, as quickly and painlessly as possible.

But the feel of her hot little hand in his overruled him. With Madison Talley, nothing was going to be quick *or* painless.

MADISON KNEW SHE WAS in trouble. Here she was, being carted off behind a man she didn't even know, headed straight for his motel room.

"Are we walking the whole way?" she asked, trying to keep up with his long, angry strides.

"It's not far."

"I guess nothing's too far in Godforsaken, right?"

"Not too."

"Uh-huh."

Did she want to go to his motel? The butterflies in her stomach were a pretty good clue that this was not a good idea. She should've invited him back to her room. But somehow that seemed even more dangerous, more intimate, more seductive. If his place was as bad as he'd made it sound, it wouldn't be very tempting to stay, would it?

Oh, yes, it would. Around Jack, everything was tempting.

All the better reason not to take him back to her hotel, with its soft bed and cool linens. At the moment, it sounded like heaven. But there was something in her—some curiosity, some spark of adventure—that made her itch to see where he lived, and what he had around him. He was a mysterious, private man, and he hadn't taken Kandy back to his motel, had he? But Madison Talley would be there.

Besides, she'd left her clothes all strewn around her own room and she couldn't face bringing Jack into that mess. It was too embarrassing.

So instead of being embarrassed, she was being hauled off to a less-than-reputable motel. Worse even than that, she was going because it was *her* idea.

"What kind of lamebrain are you, anyway?" she whispered.

Jack turned and gave her a strange look, and she decided she'd better not talk to herself any more. He already thought she was on a day pass from the loony bin.

But why? Everything she'd said to him had been so sensible, so reasonable.

Yes, definitely, *he* was the weird one, not her. He was the one who'd ambushed her in an alley, for goodness' sake. Now *that* was bizarre behavior.

Not to mention the fact that he'd scared the life out of her, that he'd breathed on her and stared at her, that he'd held his fabulous body about three-quarters of an inch away until she'd practically swooned from his heat and her heat combined.

Madison shivered. It was hard not to remember the feel of his hands on her wrists and the hot trail of his gaze as he'd looked her up and down and then some. And then he'd had the unmitigated gall to accuse *her* of coming on to *him*. Why, the thought had never occurred to her.

Okay, so maybe it had occurred to her once or twice, but she never would've acted on it. Madison did not believe in sucking up to men she didn't know.

Okay, so she felt like she knew this one, but she didn't *really* know him. This feeling of recognition, of immediate intimacy, was all a mirage. Although she had to admit, the more she saw of him, the more the imaginary and real Black Jacks began to merge in her mind. They were so alike it was almost scary.

Scary, indeed. Up ahead, he sent her a probing glance from those electrifying gray eyes and she readjusted her estimate. He wasn't scary—he was terrifying. Knee-knocking, palm-sweating, singe-her-where-she-stood terrifying.

"We're here," he announced, and Madison tried not to gulp out loud.

Excitement and anticipation threaded through her. What sort of lodging could house Black Jack properly? It promised to be very interesting.

But the place they were nearing wasn't the slightest bit interesting.

A run-down one-story motel with a blinking sign missing quite a few bulbs, Jack's place was called *El Paradiso.* Paradise? Not hardly.

Madison shuddered, but she kept behind Jack as he pulled out a key and headed for one of the nondescript doors.

"You were so hot to get here," he said softly. "I hope it was worth the trouble." And he swung open the door.

Taking a deep breath, Madison stepped inside.

Chapter Three

He knew he was being played for a fool.

The senator and his lackeys didn't bother with the likes of Black Jack Brogan unless they needed a scapegoat. Or maybe just a poor sucker so caught up in making the bad guys pay that he wouldn't care if he was being manipulated like a player piano.

"Yeah, I'll do your dirty work," he drawled, putting his feet up on the senator's polished cherrywood desk. "But you're gonna pay me, and pay me good."

But there was an ache in his gut, an ache he always got right before the shooting started.

And that's when she walked in the door.

"Get her out of here," he growled.

"Why, Jack," she purred, with an innocent smile, "you don't sound glad to see me. Didn't they tell you? We're partners on this deal, you and me. Undercover, together. Doesn't that sound grand?"

The ache in his gut erupted into a damn symphony.

Black Jack Brogan, Book # 7
Step on a Jack

Madison was simply enchanted. Not by the room. Heavens, no. It looked like any other motel room that rented for less than ten bucks a night, with a sagging bed and a chenille bedspread in a bilious shade of yellow. A crooked picture of dressed-up dogs playing poker graced the grimy wall behind the bed and a feeble chair with only three-and-a-half legs wobbled next to the window. There were four phone books stuck under the injured leg, but the chair still dipped badly on that side.

No, the intriguing thing was not the room or its pitiful decor, but definitely all the fascinating papers and maps strewn around. This room was positively rife with mysteries. She would've loved a few minutes alone with Jack's private papers, just to see what he was up to.

"Lovely place you have here," she murmured, glancing at the battle-scarred dresser and the large map of southern Texas falling over one side.

"I warned you."

"Almost paradise," she said with a cheeky grin that he apparently did not find amusing.

"The price was right."

He slammed the door shut behind her, shrouding the room in instant gloom. Too bad it wasn't the least bit cool. Madison quickly hit the switch on a chipped table lamp, feeling a little apprehensive about sitting in the dark with Jack, but he didn't seem to notice or care. He stayed where he was, lounging by the door, measuring her with his steady, predator's gaze.

With him looking at her like that, she began to overheat immediately. "Is there air-conditioning?" she inquired.

"Finicky, aren't you? You pick up a guy at a bar and then you want all the comforts of home."

Madison fanned her face. "I did not pick you up at a bar and you know it."

Without waiting for his permission she crossed to the thermostat on the far wall, next to the poker-playing dogs. She shoved the lever all the way to cool and jumped when a roar sounded from over by the window. All that noise, but only a few disheartening puffs of stale air.

Jack shrugged. "You want a drink or something?"

"Is the water okay here?" She half expected it to come out with creatures floating in it and to give her dysentery if she so much as looked at it.

"I wasn't talking about water."

"Oh. Like a *drink* drink." Well, that was hospitable of him. More hospitable than she would've given him credit for. "I'd rather have something to eat, if you have anything. I don't think I've eaten all day."

"Sorry."

"Not even a candy bar?"

"Nope. And no room service in a joint like this, either." He cocked an eyebrow. "How about that drink?"

"You know, a margarita would be really great. Something tall and cool." Madison closed her eyes and pretended she was jumping into a swimming pool full of clean, clear water. "Ahh."

"With or without the worm?" he asked, and she came back to reality.

He held a bottle of tequila in each hand, each bottle about three-quarters full. Below label level on the one in his right hand, a squirmy pink worm floated, embalmed in alcohol. If straight tequila was what he had in mind, it looked like frozen margaritas by the pool were right out.

Madison grimaced. "Without, please." She had a strong stomach, but worms were another matter entirely.

"I figured."

He handed her a tumbler full of clear liquid and she tossed back a healthy belt immediately, for courage. *Fool's courage,* she thought, as she began to cough and choke. Booze was not the answer to dealing with Black Jack Brogan or his look-alike; she'd need all her wits about her.

Jack took a long swallow right out of the wormy bottle, draining it down without a flicker of discomfort. She wasn't so lucky. Trying to stop from asphyxiating, Madison took a deep breath, but that only made it worse. The tequila was making her ears ring and her throat close up completely.

"I—I'm... dying," she wheezed. "I can't... breathe."

With a muttered oath, Jack flashed to her side and pounded her on the back. "Are you okay?"

"Yeah, I guess so." She winced. "You didn't have to hit me so hard, you know. Sorry. I keep forgetting that stuff has a kick."

"For amateurs," he said sardonically, taking another long draw as if to prove he was a pro.

Damn the man. It wasn't like she'd proposed a contest. "So, what next?" she asked, turning her back on him where he was leaning laconically against the wall.

Idly, she circled the room, casting covert glances every time she passed something interesting. But damnation, she couldn't make heads or tails of those scribbled bits of paper, and the maps had no recognizable shape, except for that one big one of Texas. She squinted at a diagram of something lying on the bed; against a big, irregular shape, it had four or five concentric circles and a small blob shaded in with dots. Hmm. What the heck was that?

"It's your party," he returned, shoving the diagram under a blank legal pad and out of her sight. "Maybe you ought to stop playing spy and make the next move. Explaining yourself might be a nice change of pace."

"Explaining myself? Oh, right. I was supposed to tell you why I was following you."

Perching on the edge of the bed, Madison smiled and took a dainty sip from her glass. This time it only blistered her lip, which was a decided improvement.

But she was still roasting in the small, stuffy room, courtesy of the liquor and the steamy temperatures outside. Not to mention Jack's presence.

"Are you going to tell me this time, or do you want to drag me off somewhere else?"

"No, this is fine," she said cheerfully.

Well, she tried to make it cheerful, anyway. It was more like husky and strained. She blew her bangs off her forehead, but the cooling effect only lasted a second. Tearing the top sheet off the legal pad, she folded it and started to fan herself briskly. Better.

Jack sat beside her on the bed, stretching out his long legs. "Quit stalling, Mad. Get to it."

"I'm not stalling." She fanned more energetically. "It's pretty simple, really, and I have a feeling you're going to be disappointed when you hear how normal and reasonable my explanation is."

"I doubt it."

"Okay, but I warned you. I told you about Black Jack Brogan, right?"

"So?"

"Black Jack is my hero—in my books, I mean. Completely by accident I saw you and it hit me." She took another sip to fortify her.

"What hit you?"

"You." She widened her smile. She knew she had a good smile; it was the only thing men ever complimented her on. So she figured she might as well get some mileage out of it. "You look exactly like my Black Jack, the way I see him, I mean. Sometimes the covers aren't so good. But you—you're perfect. The eyes, the hair, the cleft in your chin... It's truly frightening."

"I'll say," he muttered.

"Not only that, but you move like him, you sound like him, you even dress like him."

Reluctantly, her eyes moved from his dusty cowboy boots over the lean length of his disreputable jeans, lingering on the worn fly that Lola had slit with her big, old knife. *It wasn't his fly,* she reminded herself. But damn it, it sure seemed like one and the same.

She would've loved to find out if he had a button fly, like Jack, or the zipper of more modern times. But, Lord, how could she ask him that? And she sure as heck couldn't just poke around with her fingers. She felt her face flame just thinking about it. But she still wanted to know.

"Why are you looking at me like that?" he asked suspiciously.

She jumped. "Like what?"

"You're staring at my..." His brows drew together darkly. "Never mind."

Tearing her eyes away from the tantalizing bottom half of his body, she shifted her focus up to his black cotton shirt. Past his rolled-up sleeves, exposing strong, corded forearms, she saw his open collar, undone three buttons to reveal the shadow of dark hair. He had a beautiful chest, muscular and broad, but not too thick or pumped up. No, he was perfect.

And whatever the indefinable quality was that she'd tried to brew into Black Jack Brogan—savvy, sizzle, all-out steam—this guy had it. Lots of it.

Finding her voice, she said breathlessly, "Add a cowboy hat and a hand-rolled cigarette, and you could slip right between the covers of *Jack in the Saddle Again.*"

"Fascinating, I'm sure," he said, in a very cynical tone.

Madison ignored him. Black Jack was always cranky when he wasn't in control of a situation. She didn't mind. "What would you have done in my place, if you'd been living and breathing Black Jack Brogan for almost seven years and suddenly he shows up in the flesh?"

"But you knew I wasn't really—"

"Well, yes, I knew, in my head. But in my heart..." Madison paused, remembering the way he'd stared down the motorcycle toughs in the cantina, the way he'd slapped down his cards, the way he'd ambushed her in the alley. Her heart began to beat a bit faster and her mouth went dry. God help her, the tequila was starting to taste good. Absently, she murmured, "In my heart, you're him."

"No, I'm not."

"Yes, you are." She took another mouthful of tequila, letting it sit there till her tongue went numb. "Black Jack never admits his real identity. So your protests are completely in character."

"This isn't a book, Mad."

He shifted around, pulling her to face him. His eyes were steely, angry even, as he spoke in a low, forceful tone. Madison tried not to let his words and his attitude affect her, but it was too late. He was advancing on her, angling his legs around her, forcing her to sink farther back into the bed. She was scared, more of her own reactions than his assault, but he was so close, and she was trapped.

What would it be like to be kissed by Black Jack Brogan? She'd written his kisses too many times to forget, but this wasn't the same. She already felt light-headed and dizzy, and he was barely touching her, just the inside of his knees brushing the outside of hers. If he kissed her, she thought she might die right there on his bed.

And if he did anything more...

"This is real life," he continued, in that same low, potent voice, and she couldn't help but watch his narrow, wicked lips form the words.

Oh, dear. His mouth was so tempting. She licked her lip.

"Madison, are you listening?"

"Oh, yes."

He frowned. "What I do or say isn't in or out of character. It's real, got it?"

"Got it," she whispered.

"Good."

Abruptly, he stood, releasing her. Madison felt like a balloon with a puncture wound. She fell back onto the bed unsteadily, balancing her glass on her forehead. She watched him stalk to the three-and-a-half-legged chair, and then straddle it as he took another long swig from his tequila bottle. Relieved and shaken, definitely dizzy, Madison dangled her tequila glass in one hand and lifted the other one to her fevered brow.

"You thought I looked like this Black Jack guy, so you followed me." He let out a long breath. "Is that it?"

"That's about the size of it."

"Anybody ever tell you you're loose a few screws?"

"Well, no, not in so many words." She licked the last of the fiery liquid out of her glass. Was it all gone? She squinted at Jack, who seemed to be fading in and out of focus over there. "I mean, people have intimated that I'm a little different from time to time, but so what? Maybe I like being different. It's more fun than acting like some old stodgepot."

"Don't even tell me what a stodgepot is." He swore fiercely and jolted upright, knocking over the rickety chair. "I don't even want to hear it."

Madison winced at the noise the chair made as it crashed to one side, phone books and all. Jack was acting a little more than cranky at the moment.

"Madison, do you realize what a brainless, half-baked stunt you pulled? You could've been following Jack the Ripper." He stomped back over her way and she sat up unsteadily to meet the assault. "You could've been dead. I swear, most men would've murdered you by now."

"Don't be ridiculous," she scoffed. "As a matter of fact, I'm a very good judge of character. I write books that require a very sophisticated understanding of the human psyche, you know. And I would never have followed you if you were a maniac."

He ran a hasty hand through his hair, giving her a very bleak look. "Good grief, Mad. You couldn't tell a maniac if one came up and bit you. I may still be a maniac for all you know."

"Pooh." Refusing to follow that silly line of conversation any further, Madison retrieved the mysterious diagram out from under the legal pad where he'd stowed it. "What is this, anyway? Are you some kind of geologist or something?"

Before she could even get her eyes focused on the dumb thing, he'd snatched it out of her hand and stuffed it under a book clear across the room.

"You have something to hide, don't you, Jack?"

"Don't call me Jack," he ordered.

"Then what should I call you?"

"Don't call me anything."

"You're such a grouch, Jack." She waved a hand in the air and it felt curiously detached from her body. "How come I'm feeling so tipsy and you don't seem drunk at all, but you drank almost the whole bottle, and I only had one glass?"

"I can hold my liquor. You can't."

"Cram it, Jack. It's just that I didn't have anything to eat all day, which I told you, and you gave me all that tequila anyway." She narrowed her gaze, taking in the maps and strange documents around the room all over again. She might be slightly sloshed, but she wasn't stupid. This all added up to something, but what? "What is all this stuff, Jack?"

"If you know what's good for you, you'll stop your little inquisition right now."

"You already told me I don't know what's good for me," she reminded him. "Besides, this is all very intriguing. First there was the poker game, at which you maneuvered things so you could win a woman you couldn't possibly be interested in."

"Now wait just a minute—"

"Jack, Jack," she interrupted, flashing him her most knowing look. "Give me credit for a brain here. You and Kandy? Don't make me laugh."

His lips tightened into a rigid line, but he said nothing.

"So then," Madison continued, trying to think this through logically. "We know we have a setup at the poker game. We have maps and we have official-looking documents, both of which indicate research. Research means...what? A search for information, perhaps, as in an investigation. But why?"

She watched him for clues. His poker face was back in place, which was as good an answer as if he'd come right out and told her she was right on the money.

"Investigation," she repeated, really starting to build up steam. "As in investigator. Jack, you're a private investigator, aren't you?"

He said nothing. He didn't have to. No longer able to contain her enthusiasm, Madison rose to her knees on the bed and gave him a big smile.

"The biker bar—that trashy waitress—they were part of the case you're working on, right?" Again, he kept his mouth shut. But at this point, Madison's imagination was a runaway train and nothing Jack could've said would've stopped her. "Oh, Jack, this is so perfect. Even I can't believe how perfect, and I'm an optimist from the word go."

"Gee, Mad," he said, deadpan. "And I never would've guessed it, either."

"There's nothing wrong with being positive about things."

"You're a little too positive, if you ask me," he said gloomily.

"Oh, Jack, snap out of it. I'm telling you, this is going to be sensational." She scrambled off the bed and joined him over by the air conditioner, grabbing his arms and dancing up and down a little with excitement. "You're exactly what I needed, and boom, like magic, you appear."

"You needed a private investigator?"

"Not for anything personal," she assured him. "I'm not in trouble or anything. But I do have a problem."

"And I have a feeling I'm going to hear all about it, whether I want to or not."

This wasn't going well, and she couldn't figure out why. Jack should be as excited and enthused as she was. Well, he would be in a few minutes, once she explained. "It's nothing major, just what my agent Harvey calls writer's block of biblical proportions."

Jack tensed slightly. She caught only the tiniest twitch in his jaw muscle, but she knew. "Your agent's name is Harvey?" he asked quietly.

"Harvey Thornton," she told him. "He's very big in the biz. Why? Do you know him?"

"Why would I know a literary agent?"

"I don't know." She watched him a little more carefully. "Why would you?"

"No reason."

"Uh-huh." She chewed on that noncommittal answer for a few seconds, but didn't see what she could make of it. "Well, anyway, Harvey suggested I get away for a while, take a little trip, change the scenery, restoke the old brain cells, you understand."

"He sent you to Godforsaken?"

"Sort of." She shrugged. "I'm not exactly sure how I ended up in Godforsaken. I thought I was going somewhere tropical. Who knows? But the point is, I need an idea. Any idea. I'm desperate."

"But why?"

Madison positioned herself over the air conditioner, letting the cool air waft up the back of her shorts. In a defeated voice, she admitted, "I have a deadline. But I don't have an idea. I already got paid."

"But, Madison..." Jack's gaze seemed riveted to her bottom, where the jet of air was lifting her shorts, and she pulled away from the air conditioner quickly. "If you're here, you're not writing your book, are you?"

"Well, no." She sent Jack a beseeching glance. "Before I left Seattle—that's where I live—I wasn't sure I had another book in me. But, Jack, don't you see? All I have to do is follow you around for a few days, sort of listen in on your investigation, and I'm sure I'll get an idea."

"My investigation?"

"The waitress, the bikers, the maps and the charts.... What is it, Jack? Missing person? Murder? Fraud? You can tell me," she said eagerly.

"You're a nut case, Mad."

"Jack, this is karma." She wrapped her hand around his wrist, willing all the electricity she felt to zap into him, too. "Can't you feel it? This is meant to be. You and me, undercover, together. Doesn't that sound great?"

He shook her hand away. "No way."

But Madison wasn't about to be thwarted. There had to be a way to convince him. One look at the shabby room he was staying in, and the light bulb switched on in her brain. "I could pay you," she ventured. "I could pay you very well. Much better than whoever your client is now."

That caught him. She could see the little glimmer of interest in his eye. "How well?"

"What would you say to..." She really had no idea what to offer. It had been a long time since she'd read a private-eye novel. A hundred a day, maybe? "A thousand a day," she said bravely. "I'll give you a thousand a day."

"Why, Madison, maybe you did write all those bestsellers."

"I told you I did." She smiled, feeling a shiver of anticipation. She was going to be working on a case with Black Jack Brogan. "Thank you, God," she whispered.

This was better than chocolate, better than sex.... Well, better than sex with normal human beings, anyway. Superheroes like Black Jack didn't count.

"Let's toast our little project, shall we?" Jack asked, filling her glass from the wormless bottle, while he continued to nurse the other one.

"I just know my best book ever is sitting out there, if I could only get an idea." Madison took a big swallow, really enjoying the taste of the liquor for the first time. "This stuff really quenches your thirst, doesn't it?"

"Drink up," he said smoothly. "The night is young, and we're celebrating."

Looking up from her glass, she caught his sneaky grin. "You're awfully sociable all of a sudden."

"Maybe I'm enjoying the company." His smile widened, and she caught her breath. That boy had charm to spare. "So tell me, Mad, why do you write books?"

"I don't know how to do anything else."

She stifled a giggle, but her mouth was moving of its own accord, lubricated by liquor and an overwhelming need to share her life story with Jack. He was being so sweet. She began to feel so cozy.

She did have a niggling suspicion that he was trying to ply her with drink to loosen her tongue, to see if she was on the up-and-up. But she didn't have any deep, dark secrets. Almost without thinking, she rambled on, giving him the whole ragged story.

"It only took me a year to sell my first book. But it wasn't *my* book, technically."

"Why not?" Jack inquired encouragingly, and Madison kept talking and drinking and talking some more.

"You see, I wrote for Roderick Tweed, and his name went on the book."

"Now *him* I've heard of," Jack said with a tiny spark of humor.

That only infuriated her more. "Baloney!" she said vehemently. "He's a fake. It really galls me that everyone in the world is lapping up his books, and he doesn't even really write them. That nasty old recluse just comes up with the ideas and then farms them out to newcomers like me—like I was then, I mean—to do all the work and get none of the glory. Do you know he's even invited to the Literary Ball in Seattle?"

"Is that a big deal?"

"Only the biggest," she shot back. "It's a masquerade ball, and all of America's most famous authors will be there. You get to dress as your favorite literary character. And they were so stupid, so obtuse, as to invite that old fake Roderick Tweed. Not me, of course. I'm just a hardworking writer. But ol' Tweed, oh, boy. He gets an invitation, no problem."

"Sounds like you don't think much of Roderick Tweed."

"I despise him and everything he stands for." This was a subject she could spit fire on, if necessary. "Although I will admit, his famous field-research techniques do come in handy. He believes in personally scouting every place he's going to write about," she explained. "And that's sort of how I ended up in Godforsaken. I thought it might be a good place to set the new book, but that's only because I was seriously misinformed about what was here."

"And who misinformed you?"

"Harvey, I guess. Or the travel agent? I'm not really sure." Jack was becoming very fuzzy over there. Trying to focus, Madison wondered how much tequila she had actually put away. Oh, well, it didn't matter. Jack would look after her. "But back to that old reprobate, Roderick Tweed. Finally, I got so fed up being one of his slaves, that I up and escaped. I wrote Black Jack, my ticket to stardom."

"Bestseller list and all that."

"Exactly. Do you know, Jack, I was in *People* magazine? I'm a..."

But Madison couldn't think of a word. And she couldn't stand up any more, either.

"I think I'm drunk," she whispered, sliding to the floor near the edge of the bed. And then she conked out completely.

"BLACK JACK, HUH?" He leaned over her, unceremoniously grabbing her and hoisting her up onto the bed. "Well, I suppose it's as good as anything else I've been called."

He smiled to himself, inordinately tickled by Madison and her antics. She really did try his patience. Should he let her hang around for a few days? There was no doubt it would interfere with his plans, but on the other hand it sure would be amusing.

And it would also give him an opportunity to keep an eye on Miss Mad, which sounded like a dynamite idea. He'd always said, *Better the devil you know than the devil you don't.* He'd also said, *If you dance with the devil, you're going to get burned,* but he preferred not to recall that at the moment.

After pushing Madison over to one side of the saggy bed, he took off his boots, peeled off his clothes and settled in beside her. Yes, this was definitely going to be entertaining.

Chapter Four

"Who are you?" the princess whispered, barely covering her perfect porcelain form with the embroidered bed linens.

"Nobody." Black Jack pulled on his boots. "I'm nobody."

Her long curls in pretty disarray, she reclined into the soft bed. "And will I ever know with whom I've shared these memorable hours?"

Jack rose, putting Princess Henriette and her sweet charms, so recently enjoyed, out of his mind. "It'll be a whole lot safer for both of us if you never know."

"As you wish," she said easily. But he saw the spark of desire in her eyes, and he knew it was far from over.

Black Jack Brogan, Book # 10
Jack-a-Dandy

Madison felt like she'd been run over by an armored tank.

Groaning, she lifted her head, but she couldn't make out her surroundings. What time was it? What day was it? Her watch was still on her wrist, and if she squinted, she could make out the big hand at about the four and the little hand hovering around nine. 9:20.

As nearly as she could figure, it was morning, even though it was already swelteringly hot. And it appeared she'd been sleeping in yesterday's shorts and top, both now wrinkled and twisted.

Why would she have slept in her clothes? And where was she? This certainly wasn't her bed or her hotel room.

"Black Jack Brogan," she whispered, as hazy memories filtered through her aching head. This was *his* room, and she'd come here last night to drink tequila—lots of it—with him.

"Oh, my God." She sat up abruptly, immediately wishing she hadn't. Her head was pounding.

Clumsily, she stumbled to the bathroom and splashed water on her face, barely glancing at her pale, bleary reflection in the chintzy mirror over the basin, noting that one of her earrings had left a bottle-cap-shaped imprint on her cheek.

"Hung over," she said wearily, getting herself a hefty drink of water.

This was a first. She'd written Jack with hangovers before, but never truly experienced one herself. Well, there was that time after freshman-year final exams, when she and her roommate had shared a bottle of cheap wine. Until last night, when for some ungodly reason she'd thought it would be fun to match Black

Jack Brogan drink for drink with the ol' tequila bottle.

Well, she'd certainly lost the battle, hadn't she?

"You, Madison," she said, giving her reflection a sober stare, "are an idiot."

There was no answer.

"Speaking of answers," she mused. "I wonder where Jack is?"

It hadn't occurred to her until right this moment that he was nowhere to be seen this morning. Had he just dumped her into his bed and taken off?

With a rising feeling of panic, Madison dashed back into the main room. Definitely no Jack, but his stuff was everywhere.

"He didn't run off," she said with relief. At least, not for good. "And he only left this morning, because there's still an imprint of his head on the pillow on the other side of the bed." Feeling proud of her deductive powers, Madison concluded, "Ergo, he slept here, and only left this morning."

But that conclusion led to another, more disturbing idea. If Jack had slept in the bed, then he'd slept . . .

"With me. Holy smokes! He slept with me." She ran a hand through her hair, pacing next to the bed she'd shared with the man of her fantasies. "Don't panic," she told herself. "It's very clear nothing happened here. For one thing, you still have your clothes on. Yeah, that's right. My clothes are on, and he couldn't very well take them off and put them back on again, could he?"

But that was small comfort. As a matter of fact, it was sort of insulting. "He had me right here, in his bed, and he didn't even try anything?" she asked indignantly. "If the circumstances had been reversed, I don't think I would've been that noble. Of course, I wouldn't have taken advantage of him or anything," she decided, feeling magnanimous, "but I sure would've peeled his clothes off, just to get a good look."

Now that was an intriguing picture—Black Jack Brogan passed out drunk, with only Madison to unbutton his jeans and slowly, oh, so slowly, strip them off. She'd take her time, pulling them down inch by inch, revealing more and more of Jack's gorgeous muscles and beautiful skin, until she had him right where she wanted him…where she could look and she could touch to her heart's content.

"Oh, my." Fanning her face with one hand, Madison sank to the edge of Jack's dilapidated bed. "I'm sure I wrote a scene like that," she murmured. "And if I didn't, I really ought to."

She would've loved to know what he'd done all night. Had he just slept there, not even noticing that there was a woman in his bed? Or had he experienced at least a little temptation?

"Madison, get real." She shook her head at her own folly. "A man like him has got to be immune to the charms of amateurs like you."

She hunted around the edge of the bed for her sandals, and then for her purse, so she could at least comb her hair. In fact, she thought she might have a toothbrush in there, left over from a stop at the airport gift shop on her way to Texas.

But there was no purse to be found. Scanning the room, she mumbled, "Where did I leave it?"

But her search only reawakened her interest in Black Jack's papers and maps. They were everywhere. The diagram she picked up first appeared to be labeled in Spanish, which only made it more indecipherable. What in the world was all this stuff for?

More important, how long could she count on Jack being off the premises? Did she have time to give his belongings a thorough going-over, or would he embarrass her by interrupting as she pawed through his underwear?

As a matter of fact, she was very curious about where he'd disappeared to in the first place. He didn't seem like the type to run out for coffee and doughnuts. "Maybe aspirin," she murmured. Right about now, she could certainly use some. Maybe Jack had the same kind of headache she did, the kind that took precedence over everything else.

For whatever reason he'd left, this was her golden opportunity to do a little digging. Quickly, Madison abandoned the scattered documents as too complicated to deal with at the moment. She'd need several days if she was going to hope to make heads or tails of that mess.

If only she had one of those little cameras the spies always used in the movies, she could've snapped pictures of all the papers, to peruse at her leisure at a later date.

"Well, time's a-wastin'." Resolute and too curious to turn back, Madison hummed a happy tune as she started with the drawers in his scruffy dresser. It seemed the logical place, plus she was hoping to find an answer to the all-important fly-fastener question.

"Yes!" she said triumphantly. "Button fly! I knew it."

She played a finger around the small copper buttons, as once again her mind wandered to Lola snipping Black Jack's buttons. She was no Lola, but there were times she wished she were. What a kick to see herself in something black and nasty, maybe leather with tall boots, deviously drugging Jack and then tying him to the bed. Then, when he was conscious, she'd slither all over him, sliding her knife along his buttons....

"No," she told herself sternly, sticking the jeans back in the drawer. "Lola was crazy. Besides, what Lola did was in a book. You'd better get a firmer grasp of the line between fantasy and reality, Madison, or you're in serious trouble."

Of course, she was already in serious trouble. No longer content with merely talking to herself, she was standing here carrying on an entire conversation. Under her breath, she muttered, "You're losing it, Madison."

Determined to be more adult about this, she poked under the jeans, noting a few clean T-shirts and articles of clothing. The next drawer was underwear, all black briefs. "Black," she said with a sigh. "I wonder if he wore these while I was sleeping last night?"

She knew it was really rotten of her to touch the briefs, but she had to search underneath, didn't she? And if her fingers lingered a little longer than was absolutely necessary, well, who cared?

"Bingo," she said with surprise. There actually was something underneath the black pants. It felt like a packet of some sort, and she pulled it out into the light.

Now that she got a closer look, she saw that it was an envelope, folded around something small and hard, credit-card size. Eagerly, Madison opened it up to see what was inside.

"Driver's licenses," she said, bewildered, as three small plastic cards fell into her hand. "Why does he need three of them?"

The one on top definitely showed Jack in the picture, but it said his name was John Cutter, and he was wearing a beard. Number two had a mustache, and purported to be James MacChesney. She wasn't surprised to see yet another look and another name on the third one; this one was clean-shaven, with the name Jay Ballantine.

"Cutter, MacChesney and Ballantine," she reflected. "They sound so familiar. But why? And where from?" She shook her head. She couldn't quite catch the elusive memory of those names. "Maybe it just sounds like some law firm," she said with a wry laugh.

Although they had different years listed, all three licenses showed the same birthday, November 9, making him a Scorpio. That certainly fit. Scorpios were supposed to be sexy and dark, smart and unpredictable, and that was Jack or whatever his name was. In fact, she knew she'd given her own Black Jack a November birthday when she'd created him in the first place. She shivered. The coincidences were getting spooky.

Madison frowned down at the IDs. "Three driver's licenses, under different names. Why would a legitimate private investigator need to assume names all over the place?"

This was worrisome. Maybe she'd come to the wrong conclusion when she'd decided he was a P.I. Had he ever really said he was, or had she just assumed it? But most of last night was a blur, and she really couldn't remember.

She took a moment to chew on that one, but she had no real answers. When all was said and done, she came back to the same question.

Who the heck was he, and what was he doing in Godforsaken?

And then she heard the key scraping in the door. With a ferocious burst of speed, Madison wrapped the licenses back in the envelope and stuffed the whole shebang back under the underwear. She was just easing the drawer closed when Jack's lean frame and a scorching blast of sunshine filled the doorway. He was wearing black jeans and a white T-shirt. Simple and very effective. Madison couldn't help remembering the black briefs she'd so recently fingered.

"You're up," he said lazily.

Shading her eyes with her hand, she managed to say, "Just barely." Her voice was too loud, and she winced at the sound of it rattling around in her head. Damn this hangover, anyway. She swore she would never drink tequila again as long as she lived.

Thankfully, Jack closed the door, putting an end to one of her headaches. "You don't seem too perky this morning," he noted.

"I was a little surprised to find myself here this morning." Curious, she glanced at his wary expression. "Where were you off to so early?" she asked, trying to make it sound casual.

"Out and about."

Well, that was noncommittal, wasn't it? "I don't suppose you have any aspirin?" she asked hopefully, holding one hand to the side of her head where the pounding was the worst.

He smiled, and even through the haze of her muddled mind, the sheer charm of it took her breath away. "I don't think so."

"I might have some of my own, but I can't seem to find my purse." Distracted, she peered around on the floor. "It has to be here somewhere."

"There, by the chair."

"Thank goodness. I think I may even have a toothb—" she began, but then her foot got caught on one of the phone books stacked on the floor.

When she reached out to steady herself, the only thing to reach for was the wobbly three-and-a-half-legged chair, which only made matters worse. As she pitched to the floor, she knocked over the chair, three phone books and the half-full bottle of tequila Jack had been swilling from last night. Most of the liquor splashed out, liberally dousing the front of her shorts and shirt.

"Damn it," she swore from her undignified position on the floor. "Now I'm going to smell like a brewery."

But as she sniffed, she couldn't smell anything. Suspicious, she picked up the bottle, whose worm was still down there at the bottom in about an inch of clear liquid. Sticking it right up to her nose, she took a good whiff. Nothing.

Although she'd just sworn off tequila, she put the bottle to her mouth and took a small sip. No fire, no brimstone, no nothing. Madison stood up, brushing herself off, fixing Jack with a furious stare.

"Water," she shouted. "You were drinking *water* last night! I hope you know what that makes you, you heel, you creep, you...vermin."

"No reason both of us should get plowed," he returned calmly.

"No, just me." Flapping her top to air out the wet spot, Madison seethed in Jack's general direction. "Okay, mister, I want to hear this. What was the purpose of that little exercise? Were you trying to keep me from figuring out what all this junk is?"

Planning to flourish the nearest piece of paper in his face to accentuate her point, she picked up a map of Laredo and environs. Unfortunately, it unfolded itself all the way to the floor as soon as she touched it.

Dropping it, she kicked at the stupid thing and then pointedly ignored the tangle she'd made.

"Nice job."

"Thank you," she said icily, launching right back into her attack. "Was that your plan? To keep me in the dark? Or maybe you thought you'd ply me with drink and loosen my tongue? Or merely make a fool of me?"

"You do a real nice job of that all by yourself."

"That's not funny."

Moving closer, he cracked a small, cynical smile. "Just curious here, Mad, but why haven't you asked me about the most obvious theory?"

Backing up, she hit the wall. "And what would that be?"

"Maybe I thought I'd get you drunk and soften you up." Still smiling, Jack bent closer. His lips hovered about an inch away from her. Barely whispering, he added, "For a seduction."

"Don't be absurd," Madison murmured, but her eyes were on his lips. "You're not interested in…me."

"I'm not?" His voice was so low and so incredibly seductive, Madison had to fight not to sink into a little puddle at his feet. "Don't be so sure," he whispered, and he leaned in even closer, until she heard herself give out a tiny moan.

He brushed his lips against the corners of her mouth, first one side and then the other, and Madison felt herself getting warmer and more pliant. Her eyes drifted closed, as she practically oozed with suppressed desire.

"Oh, Jack," she breathed, lifting herself into his caress.

He was toying with her, not really kissing her, but not really letting her go. His mouth was tantalizingly close, just suspended there next to hers. When her tongue darted out to lick her lips, it almost touched him. Almost.

Madison was crazed. She was so close to just grabbing him and pulling him down to her mouth, anything to satisfy the terrible hunger she was feeling.

But then she remembered she hadn't brushed her teeth, and even under Jack's erotic spell she couldn't kiss a man while she had morning mouth. Besides, now that she thought about it, this was probably just another of Jack's tricks, designed to throw her off balance, to fool with her mind.

Pushing past him, she said shakily, "This is not a good idea."

"Well, if you're running scared, you know you can always back out."

She wheeled. "Back out?"

"You wanted to hire my services. . . ." He paused. "As a private detective. A thousand bucks a day was the offer."

"Oh, right." Weakly, she lifted a hand to her aching head. "I, uh, forgot."

His voice was a shade rough when he said, "Not too late to call it off. Fact is, Mad, the best things you could do for yourself is to get out of Godforsaken while the getting is good."

Madison stiffened. "I'm not calling if off. I have every intention of following your investigation and coming up with an idea for a book. That was the plan, right? See, I haven't forgotten everything." Stubbornly, she added, "A very good plan. And I'm sticking to it."

She couldn't tell from Jack's impassive expression whether he was happy or furious with her decision. If he'd thought he could scare her off by tossing that kissing thing at her, well, he was sadly mistaken.

"Okay, Mad, have it your way," he said quietly. "But if you want to follow me around, you're going to play by my rules."

"Of course." When he nodded, accepting her word, she inquired cheerfully, "So what's our next move? What are we investigating?"

"We aren't investigating anything. I am. You're just along for the ride, remember?"

She settled in on his bed. "Well, right, but still, I have to know what the case is, don't I?"

"I suppose." After watching her thoughtfully for several moments, he said slowly, "The case. You want to know about the case."

Madison smiled encouragingly. "Is it a good one? I mean, I know private eyes say most of their cases are really dull and routine, so I hope this isn't one of those."

"It is. Routine stuff." Turned away from her, he picked up and put down a few pieces of paper.

"It involves that waitress, right?" she prompted, determined to overcome his reluctance to confide in her.

"Kandy," Jack supplied. "Right. She may be a runaway, the, uh, runaway I'm looking for."

"Who's your client?"

"My client?"

"Who hired you to find Kandy?"

"Oh, right. Her father. He's rich. She's gone. So he wants me to find her."

At least things were starting to become a little clearer. "This is great, Jack! I'm already really excited."

"I'll bet."

She chose to ignore that. "So what's our next step?"

"*My* next step is to go back and talk to Kandy again," he said tersely. "All you need to do is keep your mouth shut and stay out of trouble."

She nodded her head sagely. "Right. I can do that."

"You swear you'll stay out of it? You'll let me handle Kandy?"

"Promise," she said blithely.

But it was a bit more difficult when she was actually faced with the situation. She'd raced through a shower and change of clothes at her motel, taking only a few moments to luxuriate in the coolness of her air-conditioned room before zooming back to the saloon. At least she'd have a chance to let Jack see her in something other than one grubby outfit.

After poring over her vacation wardrobe, she'd finally chosen a camp shirt and matching baggy shorts in a funky cotton print, and then exchanged last night's dangly earrings for a different pair from her collection of outlandish hoops. Today's choice was a pair made of odd lumps of recycled bottle glass.

But she'd waited too long; Jack had beaten her to the cantina. He was already there, chatting up Kandy like a long-lost friend, smiling and flashing all that Black Jack charm. Kandy looked her usual trashy self, only the halter top was glow-in-the-dark lime green this time.

Hovering in the doorway, Madison was at a loss for how to proceed. The place was practically deserted, with no bartender and only a few of the regulars snoozing here and there. The lack of customers made her goal to lay low more problematic. With nowhere to blend in, she'd stick out wherever she went.

She had to find a way to keep an eye on Kandy and Jack without upsetting anyone's applecart. Luckily, Kandy seemed to be completely absorbed in Jack, and the curvy blonde didn't even turn as Madison brazened it out, sneaking in and hiding at a small table in a dark corner. From her shadowy vantage point, she could see the two of them snuggling and giggling over there. She muttered something unpleasant under her breath. Unfortunately, she couldn't hear a thing.

"This won't do," she murmured. "It won't do at all."

But if she moved any closer, Kandy would surely see her, and it would wreck the whole thing. Madison spared a glance at Jack, who was currently doing his best to ignore her. If she interrupted his little tête-à-tête, she knew Jack would be very upset. But if she stayed over here in the corner like a good girl, her surveillance wouldn't do a bit of good.

Well, Madison Talley was not the sort of person who sat and waited for life to come to her. Resolute, she waited impatiently for her moment. Finally, Jack leaned in very close to Kandy's peroxided head, blocking his view of the rest of the room, and Madison knew her chance was at hand. As noiselessly as she could manage, she skirted around the outside of the dusty room, slipping in behind the bar very close to where Jack sat. Since there was no bartender, there was nobody to notice as she huddled under there, out of sight, but close enough to hear every word that passed between Jack and the bimbo.

"Oh, sweetie, you're so nice," Kandy said breathlessly.

"Just telling the truth," Jack drawled, in what Madison thought was a very insincere voice. "You're a dynamite woman."

Kandy giggled. "Dynamite? Wow."

"You really fascinate me, doll."

Doll? What kind of word was that for a grown-up? Madison tried not to barf behind the bar.

"Yeah, I would say I'm definitely interested." His voice became lower and huskier, and Kandy's giggles started to sound more like squeals of pleasure. What in the world was he doing out there? "But I don't want to step on any toes," he went on. "I know a woman like you has got to be heavily attached. I don't want any trouble."

Attached? What was he talking about? The squeaky guy with the blue tattoo? And why did he care? Jack's gooey approach was off the mark, if he wanted to find out whether Kandy was the runaway he was looking for.

"Tell me, sweet thing, who's my competition?"

Sweet thing! Madison couldn't believe Jack kept rolling with such tired, pathetic material.

Meanwhile, Kandy was still giggling. "Oh, well, I get around, you know, but there's nobody, really...."

"That's not what I hear," Jack returned. "I hear some rich guy from over the border has the inside track."

"Oh, you mean Carlos." Kandy snorted. "I dumped him a long time ago. Your info's kinda old, ain't it, hon?"

"So how rich is this guy? I hear he has this big hacienda, guard dogs, fancy security, the whole shot. You ever been to his place?"

"Well, yeah, but..." Kandy's voice broke off in disappointment. "I told you, there ain't nothin' between me and Carlos no more. Long time, no see. Kaputski. Finito. Got it?"

"Yeah, sure. Just curious."

What was he doing? Why ask all these questions about some rich guy and his hacienda? Madison was becoming more agitated by the minute. She simply didn't understand, and besides, she was getting cramped crouching behind the bar like this.

Jack and Miss Halter Top had now moved on to a discussion of local gossip, which Madison found a real snore. Shuffling around to get circulation back in her legs, she almost knocked over a tray of dirty beer glasses. Her heart raced, but she caught the tray in the nick of time.

"I hear there's an old story about a lost diamond mine in this area," Jack said. His voice was so studiously casual that Madison smelled a rat and pricked up her ears.

"I never heard nothin' about no diamonds," Kandy scoffed.

"Really?" Jack's chair scraped as he pushed himself back from the table. "I heard all kinds of stories. They say it's right by that rich guy's hacienda. What was his name again? Carlos. They say the diamonds are right there on his property."

"I never heard nothin' like that." Kandy was beginning to sound a bit peeved. "So, are we gonna gab about Carlos all day, or are you gonna pay some mind to me?"

As Jack hastened to lay on the baloney with a heavy hand, Madison's mind was spinning. A rich guy and his diamond mine... A pile of maps and diagrams...

She clenched her jaw. "Runaway, my foot," she whispered, making a fist in her hidey-hole behind the bar. "He's after that diamond mine and he thinks Kandy can fill in the details."

Once again, he was playing fast and loose with the truth, and Madison was not pleased. Scooting out to the side of the bar, she shifted into a place where Jack could see her if he looked directly to his left, but Kandy was still blocked.

"Psssst," Madison tried.

"Did you hear something?" Kandy asked.

"Uh, no, not a thing."

"Pssst," she said again. No response. So she waved her hands, hoping the motion would catch in his peripheral vision. He looked right at her, gave her a quelling stare, and then moved back into his sloppy sweet talk with Kandy.

"Jack," she hissed, waving her arms more furiously, trying to telegraph her need to talk to him immediately. She intended to keep up her one-woman semaphore routine however long it took.

Finally, Jack rose from his chair, pushing away and planting his boots about two inches from Madison's foot. "Kandy, sweet thing, your eye looks a little funny," he said loudly. "Maybe you should go to the ladies' room and check it out, huh?"

"My eye? There's somethin' wrong with my eye?" Kandy jumped up from the table and raced to the rest room.

Jack turned, glaring down at Madison. She stood up, brushing off her shorts, glaring right back.

"What the hell are you doing?" he asked roughly.

"I may be gullible, Jack, but I'm no fool," she shot back.

"I'm not playing guessing games with you. Spit it out."

"This is no runaway case." She crossed her arms over her shirt. "I should've realized the minute you said it, that your story was a bunch of nonsense. Kandy is about as much a rich man's daughter as I'm the queen of England."

"Madison, keep your voice down, will you?"

"No, I will not! What are you really doing, Jack?" she demanded. "Are you an investigator at all? And what do you need the bimbo for?"

"Ssshhh," he commanded, but it was too late.

Tripping back from the bathroom, the bimbo in question was blinking under a fresh coat of black eyeliner. Her wide gaze made it clear she'd already spotted them.

"Wow!" the waitress squealed loudly. "I know you!"

"You do?" they asked in unison.

"Yeah, sure." Kandy wiggled, obviously trying to dredge up some brainpower. "I saw you in *People* magazine. Madeleine Talley, right? The one who writes the books. Can I have your autograph?"

"It's Madison," she said kindly. "Madison Talley. And of course you can have my autograph."

"I knew you was somebody famous. This is so cool," Kandy enthused. "Ain't it somethin'? Like a celeb, right here in my bar."

"It's something," Jack bit out. Turning on his heel, he stalked out of the bar with steam coming out of his ears.

Madison watched him go as she signed a bar napkin for her new fan. She decided he might be upset, but she wasn't. No, all in all, she was happily discovering that real life was a lot more exciting than fiction.

"Here you go," she said brightly, handing over the autograph. Now if only she could figure out what Jack was really up to.

Chapter Five

Raising the shotgun to her beautiful bare shoulder, Maybelle pointed it straight at Jack's heart. "Don't be tellin' me no more of your lies, pretty boy. You got more tall tales in you than a gol'darn fox caught right there in the coop with feathers hangin' outta his gol'darn mouth."

Backing away carefully, trying to struggle into his pants, Black Jack raised his hands. "Now, Maybelle," he ventured, using his most honeyed tones. "Why don't we talk this over?"

A warning shot whizzed past Jack's cheek. "Ain't nuthin' to talk about. You ain't no Reb. You're a Yankee and a thief." She lowered her sights, focusing her next load of buckshot on his crotch. "And I mean to blow you to Kingdom Come."

Black Jack Brogan, Book # 6
Jack Rat

The past few days had been peaceful, with no sign of Madison. Too peaceful. He had a bad feeling about this kind of suspicious peace.

He didn't want to press his luck at the cantina, so he'd pretty much taken to ground in his motel room. All that empty time gave him the opportunity to skim through a pile of Madison's books. He figured it might offer some insight into the perplexing problem of Madison herself. Interesting reading, to say the least.

She was as smart, as creative, and every bit as goofy in her books as she was in real life. And she also demonstrated, again and again, a real knack for sticking Black Jack Brogan into the most steamy, slippery scenes imaginable with a whole slew of different women.

Poor Black Jack had been tied to a tree and covered with honey by a demented hillbilly beauty, and he'd made love upside down in a laundry cart with a prissy reporter. In fact, there wasn't much he hadn't done with that reporter, who kept popping up from book to book. But the wildest one had to be the buck-naked love scene in a haystack with an allergic princess, while a royal fox hunt raged around them.

Madison Talley had one wicked imagination. Just thinking about the haystack and the princess made him desperate for a cold shower. And it was all Madison's fault.

He lay back on the lumpy bed in his hotel room, running through a few of the trickier scenes from her books and wondering whether that kind of thing could be recreated. With Madison.

Damn her. He sat up and rubbed his temples, as if that might banish her and her hot little fantasies from his head. No such luck. The reporter and the princess were still dancing around in there, doing all sorts of nasty things. And he still had the crazy idea that he was the one man who could tap into Madison's amazing imagination. There was no end to what the two of them could create together if they really got cooking.

His own fantasies were making him nuts. They were also scaring the pants off him. He sprang up from the bed and made for the bathroom, where he stuck his head under the cold tap until he was good and drenched. But it didn't really help the ache of desire. And it only increased the nagging feeling in his gut that disaster was right around the corner if Madison stayed on the scene.

Of course, he hadn't heard a peep out of her for three days, so there was always hope that she'd gotten tired of torturing him and had gone on to greener pastures. But in his heart, he knew the idea that she'd stay away for good was only a pipe dream.

No, if he knew Madison—and God help him, he was beginning to know her very well—then she had something up her sleeve. As he thought about it long and hard, he came to one conclusion. If he was smart, he'd derail her from whatever she was up to before they were both sorry.

After finding a shirt and shaking the excess water off his head, he hoofed it to the dirty pay phone behind the cantina and then punched in a number he hadn't used in a long time.

"Hey there, Harvey," he said coolly. "How's it hangin'?"

"What are you doing calling me?" the huffy voice on the other end demanded. "I thought you retired. I thought maybe you were dead."

He let out a derisive laugh. "You knew good and well I wasn't dead, or you wouldn't have sicced the Mad-dog on me."

"The what?"

"Your girl, Madison. Come on, Harvey, don't play coy. We're both too old and tired for that."

"Well, I do have a client named Madison Talley," the man admitted grudgingly. "A perfectly legitimate client, I might add. With no connection to you or the, uh, business you and I used to share."

"Right. And I'm the man in the moon." A picture of the princess and the haystack popped unbidden into his mind and he groaned, resting his head on the top of the phone box. "Look, Harv, I know you sent her down here. I figure you thought it would be funny to let her loose on me. Quite a gag, huh? But now the fun's over, and you're going to take her back."

"I don't know what you're talking about," Harvey insisted.

But he was in no mood for deceit and denials. "Let me put it to you this way," he said curtly. "I'm trying to find something that is very important to both of us. Something missing. Something that could cause both you and me and a bunch of other folks a whole heap of trouble. I think I've figured out who's got it, and I'm trying to come up with a plan to get it back."

"Glad to hear you're making progress," Harvey put in. "We're counting on you."

"Yeah, well, I was doing okay before she showed up. But I'm not going to be able to do a damn thing with Madison Talley playing Nancy Drew right in the middle of my plans, am I?" He was at the end of his rope. Speaking very quietly, but very forcefully, he said, "I want her out of here, Harvey. Or I'll come up there myself and tie your butt in a real tight sling."

"Well, I suppose I—"

"Don't even think of turning me down," he said grimly. "Here's what you're going to do. There's a big charity bash in Seattle coming up. You're going to get Madison an invitation."

"The Literary Ball, you mean? But that's big-time," Harvey protested. "Madison isn't in that league."

"Exactly why she won't turn down the invitation."

Harvey sighed heavily. "If I can get her invited?"

"You can. And you will. Today."

"Right," the other man grumbled. "Any other miracles you want while I'm at it?"

He paused. "Now that you mention it, why don't you send me a copy of her latest manuscript?"

"You mean *Between a Jack and a Hard Place?* How'd you hear about that?" Harvey asked with surprise.

"Madison told me. How else?" He was getting very tired of this conversation. "Just send it, okay? In care of the Godforsaken post office will do."

"Can't wait for the new book, huh?" the man asked slyly. "Sounds like you're getting to be a real fan of Madison's work."

"Just trying to stay one step ahead of the competition."

He hung up before Harvey had a chance to give him any more grief about it. With any luck, Madison would be winging her way to Seattle before another sunrise, out of his hair and out of his mind completely. He sighed, a luxury he rarely permitted himself.

God help him, she'd better be gone soon. Or he was going out searching for haystacks.

THE MANUSCRIPT was waiting for him at the measly Godforsaken post office, with a note attached from Harvey Thornton. All it said was "done," but he knew what that meant.

So the hook was baited, and all he needed was for Madison to bite. She'd never pass up the company of all those highfalutin celebrity writers. Not to mention Madison's least favorite author, Roderick Tweed. What would she do if Tweed showed up?

He smiled. Old Roderick the Recluse never went anywhere, let alone to parties, so the chances were slim to none that Madison would feel the need to fling hors d'oeuvres or get into fistfights. No, he expected Madison to go, to have a great time, and never to know who'd arranged the invitation. For the first time since she'd shown up at the cantina, throwing monkey wrenches every which way, he began to relax.

Still, he couldn't resist unwrapping the package from Harvey and pulling out the packet of pages. *Between a Jack and a Hard Place*, huh? He shook his head. The only thing worse than her titles was her love scenes. He fingered page one. What would she do for an encore in this one?

Black Jack was starting to feel like an old friend, he discovered, as he thumbed through the first few pages. Not his double, as Madison believed, or even his alter ego. No, he didn't identify that closely with the fictional good guy.

But still... There was a certain amount of similarity, at least in the way Madison described Black Jack's looks. She was obviously nuts about her hero, so he supposed he should take that as a compliment. But he felt kind of odd about it, especially considering the power of Madison's imagination. When she looked at him, what was she thinking about? His pulse picked up just pondering the possibilities. Was she seeing him covered in mud? Stripped bare and tied to a tree? Dripping with honey?

He groaned. If he survived Madison Talley, he'd be doing real well.

Skimming along through her book, he was really getting interested in what would happen next. Madison had this kind of zippy, hard-boiled style that kept him flipping pages, and he found himself turning in at the town drugstore so he could sit down and read in more comfort.

Pulling up a stool at the old-fashioned soda fountain, under a couple of wheezing wooden paddle fans, he downed three glasses of ice water while he raced on through Madison's book. This one was a doozy. Trust Madison to come up with the most lurid possible situation and then throw Black Jack into a whole host of perilous plot tangles, with a cliff-hanger at the end of every chapter.

Damn her anyway. He couldn't stop reading. She had a real way with words.

"Sucker," he muttered. But he kept on reading.

"She just said she wouldn't sleep with you if you were the last man on earth," he muttered, but kept on reading.

Black Jack kissed her with anger and with passion, swiftly unfastening her tiny pearl buttons, laying her bodice open to his rapt gaze. He knew Nell so well, and he had missed her soft skin, her fiery ardor. But the kiss went on far too long, past the point of reason, and still Nell did not back away. He'd gambled that the assault would frighten her, but once more, he had underestimated Nell MacGregor.

"I have never been able to resist you," Nell said with a sultry sigh, throwing her arms around his neck.

His heart turned over, but he knew he couldn't give in. Come hell or high water, he had to make sure Nell was on the next train out of San Fransisco. He hardened his heart. "Darling Lola, I knew it was too good between us for you to walk away."

Nell went quiet in his arms. "Lola?"

He pretended to be confused. "A mistake, that's all. A small mistake. It's nothing to get upset about."

"The mistake is mine," Nell whispered, backing away toward the door, awkwardly attempting to refasten all the tiny buttons down the front of her bodice. Lifting her chin, she declared proudly, "I am

simply not the sort of person who engages in activity of this sort, and with a rogue such as you.''

Jack grabbed her wrist and pulled her up against him, hard. ''It's too late for ladylike gestures, Nell. Either you stay here and finish what you started, or get out of town,'' he growled. ''With me, lady, there's no middle ground.''

She almost relented, but Black Jack knew her too well. With effort, she pushed away, as he'd known she would. ''Farewell, Black Jack,'' she offered. And then she was gone.

''Goodbye, Nell.'' Black Jack rubbed his fist against the ache in his gut. He already missed her. But he'd had to get rid of her before things got too dangerous. He'd done what he had to do.

So why did he feel like hell?

He scanned ahead quickly. ''Holy smokes.'' He read faster.

He stopped. Madison had gone too far. This particular scene made him absolutely insane. He had the overwhelming urge to go find her, to hold her body against his, to kiss her senseless, until she melted like ice cream in a frying pan. Once he'd unleashed the power of his desire, Madison would know how much better it was to feel the passion of a real man than to plot fantasies with Black Jack.

''Get a grip,'' he told himself curtly. Deep down, he knew what was going on. He was jealous. He was actually jealous of a fictional character. All he could think about was the time Madison spent coming up with this stuff, day in and day out, living and breathing—and panting—Black Jack Brogan.

He'd never been jealous before in his life. And why start now? Madison was a goofball, a nut case, a loony tune. So why did he like her so much?

He refused to consider any of it, clinging to the notion that if Harvey had done his job right, Madison was already long gone. And what a relief that would be. He tossed some money down on the counter for the soda jerk, who'd been kind enough to let him occupy a seat for so long, and then slammed the manuscript back into the envelope.

Time for him to get back to his place and burn this thing. Time to forget about Madison for good.

His hands formed into fists as he stomped down the dusty streets of Godforsaken. He felt like a man with a mission—a mission to stop making a fool of himself over Madison Talley. A big, ugly trash can was sitting on its side in the middle of the street, but he dragged it back to the curb and dropped Madison's book inside.

Now that Madison was gone, he had plans. He was going to take a long shower, get a good, restful nap and then get back to work on the problem of breaking Carlos's security system.

But Madison wasn't gone.

"Hi," she said breezily, from the middle of his bed. "I thought you'd never get back."

Wearing a perky little shorts outfit, she sat cross-legged in the center of the saggiest part of the bed, surrounded by all of his papers. She'd rearranged them into neat little stacks, but she'd also made a hell of a mess. He stared, openmouthed, at the junk she'd brought with her. Aside from paper wads, paper clips and about ten felt-tip pens, she had an open bag of chips, a plastic container of sour-cream dip, three boxes of cookies, and a two-liter bottle of Diet Pepsi. Madison seemed to be eating all of it at once, sampling here and there with carefree abandon.

At first, he couldn't say anything. He was too much in shock.

"You're letting in hot air," she pointed out. "I finally had it sort of cool in here, and you're wrecking it."

"Sorry," he said automatically, shutting the door. What was *he* sorry for? Slowly, he edged into the room, giving her his blackest glare. "What the hell are you doing here?"

"Waiting for you." She grinned as she popped four mini-cookies into her mouth at once. "You've been gone for a long time."

Weary, he sagged back against the door. His worst nightmare was staring at him. One look at her, and all he could think about was ravishing her body. He was a worse mess than his room was.

Clenching his jaw, he asked, "Not that it matters, but how did you get in here?"

She shrugged. "I told that icky guy at the desk that I was your girlfriend. I guess he believed me."

"I figured you jimmied the lock," he muttered. "That's more your style."

"It is not." Madison went back to shuffling papers with her left hand, balancing a potato chip full of dip in the right one. "Where is it?" she murmured. "I know I had it right here."

"Madison," he warned, in a low, ominous voice. "You're getting crumbs everywhere, all over my bed, all over my papers."

"I'll clean it up," she promised, with a careless wave of a hand.

Trying to stay clear of Madison, he brushed cookie crumbs off the edge of the bed, muttering, "This is disgusting."

"Oh, lighten up, will you?" She smiled. "I'm so excited, Jack. I've finally got it all figured out."

His internal alarm system kicked into gear, and he drew back. "What exactly do you think you've got figured out?"

"You. This stuff." She rearranged herself on the bed, recrossed her legs, and then held out the box of cookies.

"No, thanks." Grim, he kept his distance from Madison and her junk-food jamboree. "What have you figured out, Mad?"

"Well, let's see."

Chewing her lip, she chose a large, flimsy sheet off one of her stacks. With a saucy smile, she held up a diagram. It was a plan of the mysterious Carlos's villa, complete with grounds and the security systems sketched in different colors to indicate actual and probable alarm locations. Of course, Madison didn't know any of that, but he did. Short of ESP, there was no way she was going to know, either.

"Well," she confided, "this looks like a sort of blueprint, like a big house and some gardens or grounds or something. It isn't marked very well, but I don't see what else it can be. Now, I don't know what all the squiggles are for—the blue ones here, and then the orange ones over here—but I can definitely conclude that this *is* a house."

He said nothing. So she'd deduced it was a house. How much else could she get right with these blind stabs in the dark?

"So," Madison continued, "I asked myself whose house this would be, to be important to your case, I mean. And I thought, whose house have you been talking about lately? And then it came to me—that rich guy, Carlos, of course. Kandy's ex-beau, the one you were asking all those questions about."

He bit down, hard, to keep himself from shouting at her. She was right, and it was making him crazier than he already was. Instead of shouting, he narrowed his gaze and kept his mouth shut, refusing to give her any ammo to verify her guesses. Not that she seemed to need any.

"I have to say, though, that I do not believe Kandy dropped him," Madison ventured. "If you ask me, it's much more likely he's the one who kayoed the entanglement, if there ever was one, which I really am not at all sure I believe, because, let's face it, Kandy is not exactly a femme fatale and a rich guy with this big mansion could certainly attract better."

"Madison," he said coldly. "Is there a point to this?"

"Of course." She smiled again, that up-to-no-good, mischief-and-merriment smile that made his bones ache. "The diamond mine."

He tried not to show his relief. "Diamond mine?" he asked coolly. "What diamond mine?"

"The one you were quizzing Kandy about."

"I don't recall anything about a diamond mine."

She sent an amused glance his way. "Jack, please, I was there, remember? There's no point in hiding it." Excited by her discovery, she scooted forward on the bed. "I see it this way—it's not *The Big Sleep* like I thought before, but *The Treasure of the Sierra Madre.* There's a diamond mine somewhere near this Carlos guy's property, and you know, I'm starting to think maybe Carlos is a drug dealer."

"A drug dealer?" he echoed. "Mad, you're losing it."

"I am not," she protested. "Okay, forget the drug-dealer thing for the time being. Here's the important part. You found out about this diamond mine, so you're gathering information and maps to find it," she said, her eyes dancing.

"Oh, really?" he drawled.

"Absolutely." Her smile widened, and he knew he was in for it. "You know what that means? You're no private eye. You're a thief!"

Chapter Six

"You lied to me, you cheated me, and you attempted to play me for a fool!" She was so angry that the ostrich plumes on her bonnet began to twitch. "Nell MacGregor is no man's fool, Mr. Brogan, I can assure you of that."

Black Jack tossed back a shot of Red Eye, neat. "I did what I had to do."

"And now I shall do as *I* must." With one jab of her parasol, Nell knocked his glass clean out of his hand. Primly, she drew herself up to her full four feet and ten inches. "From this moment forward, Mr. Brogan, I shall be your veritable shadow. There shall be no deed too small, no event too private, to escape my watchful eye. And if you should attempt any of your nefarious schemes, well, sir, let me simply say you shall regret it."

He eyed her warily. "We'll see what I regret."

And then he grabbed her and kissed her, hard.

Black Jack Brogan, Book # 1
Jack of Hearts

He was a bit taken aback. So she'd decided he was a thief. He felt sort of wounded until he realized Madison seemed to find the idea of a thief even more exciting than a P.I., if the sparkle in her eyes was any indication. She was probably already entertaining daydreams about Cary Grant as the cat burglar in *To Catch a Thief*.

"So here's the blueprint of Carlos's house," she said with enthusiasm, holding it up. "Now this—" she held up another sheet of paper "—I figure this is your geological diagram, of the minerals near the hacienda." She paused thoughtfully, tapping one finger against a big red circle. "Zoning right in on that diamond mine, right?"

What she was looking at was an aerial overview of the area in question, marked with possible landing strips for a small plane, but he decided not to wreck all her fun by telling her the truth.

"Come on, Jack, I know what's going on," she persisted. "There's no reason to hold back now."

"Be quiet, Madison," he said evenly. He set one knee on the bed, leaning in far enough to make her quickly back up to the headboard. He edged in closer. Her eyes widened, and he knew she was wondering how close he was planning to get.

There was a decided advantage to having read her books, to getting better acquainted with ol' Black Jack, even though the memory of those steamy pages started sending hot sparks to the wrong places all over again. But now he knew what popped Madison's buttons, and he got a perverse sort of pleasure out of using the information. Taking the offensive for the moment, he bent over her all the way, pressing the length of his body against hers, scattering cookies, making Madison gasp with surprise and apprehension as he pulled her into his arms.

"Be quiet, Mad," he said again, breathing the words into her mouth. Her eyes fluttered closed as her lips parted. She raised her mouth toward his. She had a sweet, vulnerable mouth, and he was very tempted to tighten his embrace, to pull her under him, to try out of few of his dark fantasies.

But with a fierce imposition of self-control, he snatched both documents out of her hand and dropped her. As she sank down into the remains of her junk-food picnic, like a Victorian lady with the vapors, he gathered up the rest of the stuff she'd been snooping through. "You've meddled where you don't belong for the last time," he said grimly, stuffing the papers into a hasty stack. "The best thing you can do is get out now, while the getting is good."

"Get out? Are you crazy?" Madison regained her spirit quickly. She scrambled off the bed, challenging him as he savagely shoved all the papers out of sight under a heavy tome about Texas legends. "I hired you, in case you forgot. Well, you're still hired, mister! And I'm still planning on getting my money's worth."

"What?" He turned around and glared down into those ridiculously pretty eyes of hers, alight with green fire, framed with spiky black lashes. He looked away.

"Yessirree," she insisted, smacking a fist into her palm. "You're going to work for your money."

"Madison, look. I hate to bring up reality, since it's not your best subject. But you haven't paid me one red cent." He felt like shouting, but he kept his voice level. Barely. "So tell me," he said tersely, "what money is it I'm working for?"

"Oh." Her cheeks flamed, and he was glad she had the grace to be embarrassed. "I'll, uh, write you a check," she offered, lifting her chin and acting very dignified and proper all of a sudden. "I'll get my purse."

"I don't want your—"

"No, no," she insisted. "I said I'd pay and I will."

"But, Madison, I don't want the money. Or the job!"

She ignored him. After searching for a few minutes, she found her bag next to the bed and began to root around in it. A huge woven rucksack of a thing, it looked like a Peruvian grocery bag. Madison pulled out a hairbrush, a small notepad, a large FiloFax, a full-size manila folder brimming over with paper, about fifteen pens, and finally, a checkbook.

"Well, let's see," she mused. "Half a day on Tuesday, when we were interrogating Kandy... And I guess that's it. So five hundred, right?"

He wasn't going to let her pay him anyway, but fair was fair. "What about the night before, when I baby-sat you all night long?" he demanded.

"That was your fault, not mine," she said huffily. "You're the one who got me plastered while you were chugging *water.*"

His gaze narrowed in her direction. "I still put you up for the night. Kept you safe from wolves and coyotes."

"You're the only wolf I know," she returned.

"I didn't touch you," he snapped.

"I know."

He glowered down at her until it became clear she wasn't giving in. "Guess I should've tossed you out in the street, huh?" He shook his head. "And what about today? You're sitting on my bed, making a shambles of my place, and that should count."

"You're being ridiculous." But she raised a hand in defeat. "Okay, okay, I'll give you twelve hours for Monday, six for Tuesday, and six for today. Which is extremely generous, I might add, because I didn't use nearly that much time. That makes twenty-four hours, or one whole day, for one thousand dollars."

"Who do you know who works a twenty-four-hour day?"

"If you're going to be picky, I'll make it two days. But that's my final offer."

"I deserve time-and-a-half for combat pay," he muttered.

"Well, you're not going to get it." Waving a pen over her checkbook, she glanced up at him. "Who do I make it out to?"

Devious little thing. Was it all a ruse to find out his name? Or had she just decided to make the most of the opportunity when it presented itself?

"I want cash," he said coolly.

"Oh, come on." She tapped her pen impatiently. "You'll have to wait for cash. I can give you a check right now. Besides, you don't have to give me your real name. What about Ballantine and Carter? Or was it Cotter? No, wait—Cutter, that's it. And Mac-whatever-it-was. I saw the driver's licenses, Jack, so I know you've got three identities all lined up to choose from. Why don't you just use one of those?"

He stared.

"So, which one?"

"You little snoop," he said harshly. "You rifled my drawers."

"You knew I would. I mean, what did you expect me to do? You left me alone here for hours." She frowned. "Really, Jack, any normally curious person would've taken a look around, just to see what they could find out."

Abruptly, he sat down on the bed. Good God, he was in trouble. Madison knew about his three favorite identities, plus she knew he was zeroing in on Carlos's house. This was a disaster. He could never remember botching a case this badly in his entire life.

"Sloppy," he muttered. "Good thing you retired, bucko, because you can't hack it anymore."

"Excuse me?"

"Nothing." He shook his head again, this time to forcibly clear his mind. He had to think.

"So, are any of those the real one? I mean, I think I read that criminals do stay on the general theme of their real names. I thought about using a pseudonym, when I started writing, and I actually did pick something with the same initials. What was it?" She chewed her lip, but didn't pause long enough for him to jump in and cut her off. "Melissa, Marjorie, Mallory... No, wait, it was Marlowe. Marlowe Tamburlaine, for that literary sound. But my agent, Harvey, thought it was a really dopey choice, and he convinced me to stick with the real thing." She brightened. "So which one of yours is the real one?"

"All of them," he shot back.

"Okay, okay, so you don't want to tell me." She perked up. "How about if I just use Cutter? I think that's the one I like best. It has a nice hard edge to it, you know, like *Cutter and Bone.* Isn't that a movie?"

"Madison," he warned. "I told you I don't want your damn check. I meant it."

Reluctantly, she stuck her checkbook back into her purse. "Okay, okay, no reason to snarl at me."

"I swear, Madison, one more word out of you, and I'll..."

She raised an eyebrow. "You'll...?"

"I'll kill you. With my bare hands." He smiled, a thin, evil smile he borrowed from every movie bad guy he'd ever seen. Since Madison was so enamored of the movies, maybe this would shut her up.

"Pooh. You wouldn't kill me."

So much for that theory.

Meanwhile, his mind was racing. He'd thought he could amuse himself with her for a while, but keep her safely on the outside, playing cops-and-robbers. And when that didn't work out, he'd thought he could simply send her away. Wrong again.

She knew too much. Too much not to interfere with his plans in a major way, unless he took care of her right now.

"Look, Jack, it's no problem. I can help you. It will be great fun."

"Right." He pressed his lips into a grim line. No question. He had to get rid of her. But how?

"When do you want to go looking for the diamond mine?" she asked politely. "What should I wear?"

"What do you wear?" He really was going to do something drastic if this kept up. "Enough," he said flatly. Unless he thought of a better plan, he was going to strangle her within the next three minutes.

Unfortunately, if he put his hands on her, the odds of throttling her dipped down to next to nothing. No, once he touched her, his hands would be on her for a long, long time. Stroking, caressing, holding her and touching her....

He clenched his hands into fists. They'd both end up breathless, but there wouldn't be any strangling going on. Murderous intentions or not, *he* would be the one in danger. In danger of blowing this job, which was too important to screw around with. Not to mention in danger of losing his mind.

She had to go. While he still had any hope of controlling himself.

Trying to think of a way to get her out of his hair reminded him vaguely of Black Jack. The words from Madison's book echoed in his mind.

Could he use sex to get Madison to do what he wanted? It was low-down, but it just might work.

"Madison," he said softly, "I don't want to talk about this anymore."

"No?"

"No," he whispered, meeting her on her side of the room, trailing a negligent finger down her bare arm. She shivered, and he liked the feel of it. When her eyes went wide like that, when her sweet lips parted slightly, she looked like the answer to a lonely man's prayers. "Ever since I first met you, I've wanted only one thing."

"And, uh, which one would that be?"

"You. I want you," he said hungrily, bending down to nip her ear. But first he had to disentangle the wire of today's bizarre choice of earring, some configuration of feathers and plastic fish. Pulling it out, he gazed down at it. "What the heck is that?"

"Fishing lure," she said breathlessly, taking it out of his palm and tossing it over her shoulder. "Forget about it."

That wasn't hard. Now, he bit gently on the pretty pink lobe of her ear. "I want you," he said again, purposely puffing warm air into her ear. "Every time I look at you, it's all I can think of."

"You're kidding," she mumbled, but there were sparks of fire in her eyes and she was trembling.

He kept his voice low and dark. "Do I look like I'm kidding?"

God help him, he'd never been more serious in his life. The trick was convincing himself he was faking it, when he knew damn well he wasn't.

"I don't kn—" she whispered, but he cut her off before she had a chance to say more.

Backing her into the wall, he trapped her between his arms, covering her mouth with his. It was a quick assault, but it wasn't painless. Not for him.

He hadn't meant to take it this far, to nibble at her, to drink her in, to lose himself in the sweet, moist sanctuary of her mouth, until he was aching for more. But she was too hot, too open, and he couldn't hold back. Bracketing her face with his hands, he pulled her closer, changed the angle of the kiss, pushed deeper. If this was a battle, he was losing.

He'd expected Madison to have unexplored depths, but these waters were way over his head. For a nut case, she packed a hell of a punch. He couldn't remember getting mixed up with any woman with this much energy, this much raw passion that she didn't seem to realize she was generating.

Almost without realizing it, he edged a few steps backward, drawing her with him, ever closer to the bed. He took a moment to break away, to breathe, before he ripped the mustard yellow bedspread from the bed, scattering the spread and Madison's snack assortment onto the floor with one violent shove. And then he fell back onto the sheets, holding Madison close, pulling her with him.

She was kissing him back as urgently as he was kissing her, and he was having a hard time remembering he was doing this for a reason. He wanted to make love to her. Now.

His mouth trailed kisses everywhere he could reach, on her neck and her throat, across her cheeks and her eyelids, until she moaned with pleasure. Madison grabbed him by the shirt, unbuttoning him and slipping her hands inside to stroke his chest and his back. He swore out loud. What the hell was she doing?

She was supposed to be running scared because he was pushing too hard. Instead, she was hotter than he was.

Knocking her hands away, he fastened his mouth on hers again, wrapping her slender arms around his neck. His forehead rested on hers as his fingers moved to attend to her buttons, sliding each one through its hole with excruciating precision. And when he'd undone them, one by one, he slipped her shirt back, revealing small, firm breasts barely covered in a lacy black bra.

She was beautiful. Softly, slowly, he brushed his mouth down the slope of her neck, over her shoulders, under and around the thin black straps of her bra, over the tops of her breasts. Even as he made himself take it slow, his blood was racing, and he could feel the pulse of her desire beating even harder when his mouth touched the skin over her heart.

She lay back into the saggy bed, her mouth bruised from his, her eyes huge and dazed. "Black Jack," she whispered. "Make love to me."

"I'm not Black Jack," he said roughly.

But she reached for him, looping her arms behind his head. "Close enough."

"No," he said pointedly. "Close doesn't count. *I'm* making love to you, not Black Jack, not anybody else. Just you and me. Can you handle it?"

"Oh, yes," she whispered. "Oh, yesss."

But could he? He was supposed to be scaring her off, and all he was doing was binding her even closer to his side. He couldn't do this. With cold, heartless reason uppermost in his mind, he retrieved the memory of her book, of how exactly Black Jack had gotten rid of Nell.

Black Jack had purposely called Nell by another woman's name.

He took a short breath. Could he be that much of a jerk? With a woman like Madison lying in his bed, ready and willing, could he strike that kind of dirty, rotten blow?

He didn't have a choice. He hardened his heart, pulling Madison closer. "Darling," he whispered, nuzzling her neck. "Darling Kandy."

Madison went quiet in his arms. "Kandy?"

He pretended to be confused. "A mistake, that's all. A small mistake. It's nothing to get upset about."

"A small mistake?" Madison cried out in a strangled little voice. "Are you insane? You call me *Kandy* and you think it's no big deal?"

She was flaming now, and he had no way to stop her. In the book, when faced with this scenario, Nell had said something sweet and ladylike and then left. None of this histrionics stuff. Trust Madison to go fiction one better.

"A small mistake," she said again, with more acid this time, and she smacked him on the chest with one small fist. "Yeah, well, the mistake was mine, bucko." She backed away toward the edge of the bed, awkwardly attempting to refasten the tiny buttons down the front of her shirt. Lifting her chin, she declared proudly, "I'm not the kind of bimbo who fools around at all, and especially not with a creep like you."

He grabbed her and pulled her back up against him, hard. If she wanted Black Jack, she was going to get him. With the words of his fictional rival ringing in his brain, he quoted, "It's too late for ladylike gestures, Madison. Either you stay here and finish what you started, or get out of town." He gave her a sharp, cynical smile. "With me, lady, there's no middle ground."

Her mouth fell open, and for a minute he thought she'd recognized her own words. Instead, she shook her head. "What a bunch of macho junk," she protested. "Who writes your dialogue?"

You wrote my dialogue, he wanted to retort, but he held his tongue. "Are you staying here and finishing?" he asked. "Or are you getting out?"

With effort, she pushed away, as he'd known she would. "Goodbye, Black Jack," she offered. And then she was gone.

That was the way it was supposed to happen. Except that she wasn't gone. She was standing at the foot of the bed, smashing her snacks and the rest of her things into her big, ugly tote bag, looking like she was on the verge of tears.

"Don't worry about me," she said, in a brave little voice that made him feel like a real heel. Well, hell, that was the effect he was going for, wasn't it?

"I'm not going to miss you at all," she continued. "As a matter of fact, I was thinking of leaving anyway." She fished a square envelope out of the depths of her purse. "I've been invited to the Literary Ball. Harvey was so thrilled for me that he even sent me a plane ticket."

He gave her a half smile. "And you were going to pass that up to play *The Big Sleep* with me?"

"No," she said absently. "Not *The Big Sleep. The Treasure of the Sierra Madre.*"

"Right." He ambled to his feet, jamming his hands into his pockets and turning his back on Madison. He simply couldn't watch her acting all woeful and self-righteous. "So when are you leaving?"

"Tonight. I have to leave soon if I'm going to get to the airport on time." She sighed. He'd never heard Madison sigh. It was much too pessimistic a sound for her. "So I guess this is goodbye."

"Goodbye, Madison."

As she and her purse and her three boxes of cookies finally cleared the door, he rubbed his fist against the ache in his gut. He already missed her. But he'd had to get rid of her before things got too dangerous. He'd done what he had to do.

So why did he feel like hell? And why did he feel like a pale imitation of Black Jack Brogan?

He crossed to the window, peering around the curtain into the street outside, watching until he was sure she was gone. But she strode purposefully down the dusty road, lugging her tote bag, not looking back. He shoved the curtain closed.

His little ploy had worked like a charm, just like it did in *Between a Jack and a Hard Place.* It only made it worse that it was a stolen idea.

"Score one for Black Jack," he said mockingly, taking a good-size belt out of the bottle of real tequila this time. Now at least he'd have something to blame that churning feeling in his stomach on.

As he paced back across the room, he stepped on Madison's fishing-tackle earring, the one he'd taken out when he was nibbling her ear. "Hell," he muttered, picking it up and crushing it in his fist. All he could think of was that pretty pink ear, and his teeth biting down, ever so gently.

Madison had been in a swoon, in a daze, and those sparkling green eyes of hers had gone dark with passion. What a fool he was. They could've had a hell of a time together, and he'd let her get away. He'd pushed her away.

"Kandy," he said with a snort. As if any woman in her right mind would believe Kandy was a threat.

He kept on drinking, until it was dark and gloomy in his room, until Madison was surely on the way to her plane, just a memory for the good folk of God-forsaken. She was finally gone, and he ought to be celebrating.

"Come on, get yourself together," he commanded himself, and he roused himself enough to get over to his dresser. Time was a-wastin'. He still hadn't double-checked the accuracy of the alarm-system diagram, and he'd be damned if he'd barge onto Carlos's turf without being absolutely sure of what he was doing.

But he couldn't find the right diagram. In fact, he couldn't find a whole lot of things. The blueprint, the map of landing strips, a map of Laredo, even his three driver's licenses.... All gone.

"Madison," he said between clenched teeth. "The little rat."

The whole teary goodbye had been a scam, just to get him to turn his back long enough for her to steal him blind. With a muttered oath, he wondered whether he could catch her. Or was he going to have to go all the way to Seattle to retrieve his files?

He threw some clothes into a small leather bag, cursing Madison's name all the way. Played for a fool at his age. Damn.

"Damn that woman. And damn Harvey, too, for sending her down here." That was one good thing. Since he had to go to Seattle anyway, he'd have a golden opportunity to smash Harvey's face in at the same time.

But if his mood was grisly, his packing was worse. He had no idea what the heck he'd stuck in there, but it was too late now. Satchel in hand, he charged out the door.

Boom. He heard the noise, a dull thud, at the same time he felt a sharp pain in the back of his head.

"What th—"

But he got no further. It was lights out for Black Jack.

Chapter Seven

Everyone in the ballroom was staring. At him. "Who is he?" they whispered.

Black Jack tightened his jaw. He hated the damn silk and frills of his evening suit, hated this fancy soirée, hated the snooty Brits who were funneling money and supplies to the Rebs. If these foppish toffs had kept their noses out of Yankee business, Black Jack could've been back home where he belonged, with a horse under him and a good shot of whiskey in his hand. Instead, he was making a spectacle of himself. And in the bargain, he was losing his chance to finger the blockade runners.

"Why, I do believe it's my cousin Alistair, from the colonies," a very lovely young woman with dancing eyes offered loudly, linking her arm through his.

"Is he really your cousin, Miss Wickham?" an elderly duchess asked coldly. "How very singular."

Well, he was game if she was. "Alistair Wickham, at your service," he said coolly.

And without further ado, the Alistair caper was begun.

Black Jack Brogan, Book #8
Jack Be Nimble, Jack Be Quick

Madison was nervous. It was her first Literary Ball, and she wanted to do everything right. But all of her personal heroes were here and it wasn't easy to quell the butterflies, to pretend to be as self-assured and socially slick as everybody else.

First of all, there was the problem of her costume. Guests at the Literary Ball were required to dress as their favorite fictional characters. From her vantage point near one of the huge refreshment tables, Madison had spied a set of Brothers Karamazov; Captains Hook, Ahab and Nemo; Zorro and Don Quixote; and an even dozen Scarlett O'Haras. There were multiples of Maid Marian, Anna Karenina and Cinderella, along with at least two Little Red Riding Hoods and their dates, the Big Bad Wolves.

As a lovely blonde in Grecian garb swept by, Madison gave her costume a covetous glance. "Helen of Troy. Now why didn't I think of that?"

Well, she'd wanted to be different, hadn't she? She'd accomplished that much. There might be ten Alices running around, even a White Rabbit or two, but she was the only Mad Hatter at the Literary Ball. Unfortunately, being different only got you so far.

With an oversize top hat, a huge polka-dot bow tie, white gloves, a bright blue swallowtail jacket and baggy orange-and-yellow checked pants, she looked more like she belonged on the vaudeville stage than at a fancy costume ball. It was no wonder she kept wishing she'd chosen something prettier and more elegant, like that lovely Guinevere over there, chatting with the crew from a local TV station.

And then there was the issue of her tardy invitation. As nearly as she could determine, everybody else had received their invitations weeks ago. She couldn't help but feel out of sorts that she'd been asked at the last possible moment. She'd barely had time to think of a costume, let alone find one. Of course, she would've had an extra day if she hadn't tarried with Black Jack—or whoever he was—but she wasn't sorry she'd done it.

Madison smiled into her glass of punch. She would've loved to see the look on his face when he realized she'd made off with his maps and papers. It was a pretty sneaky thing to do, stealing his things when his back was turned.

But he'd deserved it. Calling her Kandy. Why, she bristled again just thinking about it. "Kandy," she muttered with contempt. "Kandy!"

"Why so grouchy, little Madison?" a sly, snaky voice asked at her elbow.

She knew who it was before she turned. "Marley," she said without enthusiasm. "I should've guessed what you'd come dressed as."

"Of course you should've." Under his trademark mane of wild hair, Charles Marley preened, adjusting the heavy chains clanking around his neck. "Marley's Ghost, of course."

"Of course." Now that she looked more closely, she noticed unusual signs of luxury, for a ghost. Instead of tattered sheets, Marley appeared to be wearing gray silk, hand tailored to fit his portly frame, and costume or not, his wrist was wrapped in a heavy platinum Rolex dripping with diamonds.

What was with Marley? He'd come up through the ranks like she had; he'd even ghostwritten for Roderick Tweed like she had. So where was he getting all the money?

"What did you do?" she asked, pointing at the watch. "Knock over a bank?"

"My books are selling like hotcakes," he said happily. "Some of us have the touch." He smirked. "And some don't."

Madison manufactured a thin smile. "My books are selling just fine, thank you." Which was perfectly true. Of course, she would've said it even if it weren't, just to wipe that creepy grin off Marley's face. Cocktail chatter with her peers tended to decline into exaggeration and one-upmanship rather quickly. "Still," she told Marley, "you have four ex-wives and a passel of kids to support, if I'm not mistaken. You're always moaning about money."

"It's only three ex-wives," he said peevishly, sloppily snagging the olive out of his martini between two fat fingers.

"Maybe four," breathed a veiled Scheherazade, who popped in with enough dexterity to hijack Marley's olive. "Hi, Madison." She shifted her veil to the side to eat the olive, revealing the bottom half of another familiar face.

"Sheri," Madison said with delight. "I haven't seen you in ages!"

Sheri was another one of the old gang, that bunch of five or six struggling writers who'd toiled to produce Roderick Tweed's masterpieces back in the bad old days. Like Madison and Marley, Sheri had left the Roderick Tweed salt mines years ago to strike out on her own, under her own name. But unlike Marley, with his hard-boiled police procedurals, and Madison, flush with Black Jack Brogan's success, Sheri was still struggling. Even if she was the best writer among them.

"This is a surprise," Madison added. "I didn't expect to see you here."

"Don't say it," Sheri laughed, swishing her hips in her gauzy Arabian Nights outfit. "Not upscale enough. Me and my lowly kiddie books. But tonight, I'm Marley's date, not just another wanna-be."

"Marley's date?" Madison glanced back and forth between them. She'd always liked Sheri, but Marley was another story. Pushy, arrogant, and not all that talented as a writer, he pushed the edge of Madison's tolerance after about three minutes.

"I wanted to see the stars," Sheri said mischievously, leaning in closer to whisper confidentially. "Did you see Michener? And Barbara Cartland is here, do you believe it? It's rarefied air we're breathing tonight, Madison. Even if I don't fit in."

"You do fit in," Madison protested. "Especially your costume. I wish I'd thought of that."

But Sheri waved away the compliment. "Marley bought it for me, so I don't deserve any credit. But it is pretty, isn't it?" She fluffed the gauzy pants, shot through with gold threads.

"It's beautiful. Want to trade?"

"Oh, Madison, don't be silly. Your costume is adorable."

"I'd rather be beautiful and exotic than adorable," Madison said woefully. "Any day."

Sheri lifted an eyebrow. "I'd rather sell books. I feel like the wicked stepchild here tonight, no matter what I'm wearing."

"But your books are great!" Madison protested. "They ought to be valued a lot more highly than most of these puffed-up old frauds' work."

"Like Roderick Tweed?" Marley asked dryly, taking time out from snarfing cheese puffs to actually participate in the discussion.

"His books are great, too." Madison sent them a wide smile. "After all, *we* wrote them."

"Exactly." Sheri leaned over to snag a grape on the refreshment table. "There wouldn't be a Roderick Tweed without our blood, sweat and tears."

A passing Bo Peep, complete with a small, cuddly sheep under one arm and a long, curved crook in her hand, poked her head into their conversation. "Did I hear the name Roderick Tweed?" she asked, and the others nodded reluctantly. "Did you hear the news? He's coming tonight!"

"No!" they chorused.

"Yes," Bo Peep returned in a gossipy tone. "Nobody's seen him in years, of course, I mean, he's a total recluse, worse than J.D. Salinger. But I have this friend on the invitation committee, and she says they sent him one, of course, even though never in a million years did they expect him to come. Well, no surprise, no response. But then, like yesterday, suddenly he says he's coming!"

"No," the others said again.

"Yes! And my friend was, like, scrambling to get his invitation and name badge together on such short notice. She's hovering at the reception table to see him as soon as he sets foot in the hotel."

"*If* he shows up," Marley put in sourly.

"He said he would," Bo Peep returned. Handing Madison her sheep and her crook, she hastily filled a plate with strawberries and small pastries, and then began to chow down as she spoke. "Why would he say he was coming and then not?"

"But no one's seen him in years," Sheri argued, her eyes wide. "No, make that *ever.* No one's ever seen him, have they?"

"Roderick Tweed, out of hiding..." With a positively surly expression on his round face, Marley paused to dramatically shake his thick mane of hair. "I, for one, refuse to believe it."

"What'll he come dressed as, Father Time?" Madison joked. "He must be in his nineties."

"No." Cinderella seemed positive. "I've heard he's only about sixty."

Madison laughed. "But they were saying that back when he sold his first book. Which would've made him at least eighty when we worked for him." She appealed to her fellow Roderick Tweed ghostwriters. "Right?"

"I don't know. I never really heard how old he was." Sheri shrugged. "I never really cared."

Marley's piggy eyes narrowed. "All that mattered to me was how hard I worked and how little credit I got. His name was on the books, and I got nothing."

"You got paid," Madison reminded him. She took a swallow of her punch. "And in those days, that was enough."

"No more," Marley said with satisfaction. "And one of these days, Roderick Tweed will be working for me."

Sheri giggled, cuffing her date on the arm good-naturedly. "Don't count on it, Marl. Don't count on it."

"You guys wrote for him?" Bo Peep took a gander at their name tags. "Oh, sure, Charles Marley. Precinct 212, right? And Madison Talley." Her perky little face brightened. "I love Black Jack Brogan. I didn't know you wrote Tweed books. What a put-down, huh?"

"Thank you," Madison said dryly, choosing to take the compliment and ignore the rest of it.

"But you, hmmmm..." Bo Peep concentrated on Sheri's name tag. "No, I've definitely never heard of you.'' She lifted her dotted-swiss shoulders, and then confided, ''I write true crime myself. You know, *His Brother's Killer, She Deserved to Die, Death Pact,* those. I've had four TV movies. Great stuff.''

''Sounds like it,'' Madison said faintly, but Marley looked very interested. Probably angling for a mini-series of his own.

But before Marley could get out any probing questions, Bo Peep suddenly clutched Madison's arm and demanded, ''What's that?''

''What?'' Madison turned, as the others did, curious to pick up whatever vibrations were freaking out Miss Peep. There was a certain amount of rustling, loud whispering and scrambling happening near the entrance to the ballroom.

''Something's going on over there.'' Bo Peep stuck her hands on her hooped hips. ''I bet it's Roderick Tweed. I bet he's here. And I'm going to see for myself what the old recluse looks like. Howard Hughes is my bet—lots of hair and three-foot fingernails. You just wait and see. I'm going to get another book out of this.''

With determination, Bo grabbed back her sheep and her crook and set out for the thick of things, but the others stayed where they were, fiddling with their glasses and their finger food. Miss Peep seemed to be stalled, several clumps of people away, unable to get any closer to the source of the disturbance.

''Let me through!'' she steamed, but nobody made a path for her.

"Well, are you guys interested in seeing him?" Sheri asked gingerly. "I suppose we could sort of shimmy over that direction."

"Well, I would be—"

"It's not him," Marley snapped, cutting Madison off. He perched on tiptoes, almost spilling his martini as he struggled to see over the crowd.

"Want us to give you a boost, Marley?" Madison inquired. She hitched up her baggy pants, which had a dangerous habit of slipping. "Maybe you could see better if you stood on the table."

"Hmm? No, no." He waved her away, paying no attention to her sarcastic cracks. "No, it's not him." Marley sank back to his feet. Pulling a handkerchief from somewhere out of the voluminous folds of his slinky ghost costume, he mopped his wet brow. "It's some scruffy cowboy guy. Looks like he just walked out of Marlboro country. I have no idea why he's causing such a ruckus, but he's no Roderick Tweed. I'd bet my life on it."

And then, mumbling something about the little boys' room, Marley trundled off, still looking like a storm cloud in his big, loose gray ghost outfit.

Madison barely noticed the hasty exit. "Cowboy type?" she said slowly. She was beginning to have a bad feeling about this.

"I can't see," Sheri complained, shifting around for a better view. "I don't get it. Why is everybody so excited over one cowboy? I already saw Tonto and the Lone Ranger. Aren't they cowboys?"

"That guy's more a lone wolf than a lone ranger," a young woman dressed as Tinkerbell tossed out, in a raucous voice that totally ruined her sweet, virginal little fairy image.

Madison's dark suspicion got darker. Cowboy. Lone wolf. Here. "It can't be," she murmured.

"Who *is* that?" The whisper slithered across the ballroom, echoed nearby by a cluster of Cinderellas.

Bo Peep came careening by, almost knocking over a whole tray of raspberry tarts with her crook. "I swear to God," she declared. "I saw him up close. It's Black Jack Brogan."

"Ohhhhhh," they all said around her, with a rush of interest and enthusiasm that made Madison dizzy.

"You mean he's dressed as Black Jack?" Sheri asked. "Isn't that great, Madison? Somebody came dressed as your character."

"No, I mean he *is* Black Jack Brogan," Bo insisted. "That guy's not dressed as anything. He just *is*."

"I don't get it," Sheri said again.

Bo Peep sighed. "Wait till you see him. The look in his eye... The way he walks, all kind of loose hipped and rangy... Well, he's got *it*. Trust me."

"Oh, dear." Slipping into a chair propped next to the refreshment table, Madison pulled off one of her gloves and raised a cool hand to her forehead. "I didn't think he'd follow me. Maybe it's not him." But if it wasn't him... Could there be *two* of them?

"Oh, my goodness." Sheri's voice rose an octave, and Madison knew her friend had caught her first glimpse of the mystery cowboy. "He's fabulous," she whispered. "Black Jack in the flesh. Madison, what do you think of him?"

When Madison didn't answer, Sheri glanced down at her friend. "Are you okay? Your face is as white as your gloves."

She shoved both gloves into her jacket pocket. "I'm, uh, fine."

"You don't look fine," Sheri persisted.

"I'm fine."

But he was getting nearer. She could feel it. And she wasn't fine at all. Sort of like the parting of the Red Sea, a path was being cleared for him as he stalked through the gaily dressed crowd. If she listened closely, Madison could hear his footfalls, stomping ever closer, and she could hear the rustle of costumes, as people drew back out of his way.

"I'm dead," she whispered. If Jack was here, if he was on the warpath, then he was surely going to kill her.

She didn't dare look up. But Sheri announced, in a strangled tone, "Madison, he's heading this way. He's heading right for you!"

Cowboy boots, their leather dusty and cracked, stopped right under her eyes. As she kept her gaze straight down, she saw the tips of his boots and the pale bottom edge of his worn jeans.

"Hello, Mad," he said, in a voice that was maddeningly calm. "Nice outfit."

She grimaced, wishing once again she'd worn something else. "Why not Elizabeth Bennett?" she muttered. "Why not Jane Eyre? Why not Titania?"

"What are you carping about?"

"I'm not carping," she said angrily, rising to her feet and lifting her chin so she could look him in the eye while she argued with him.

There was no way in the world she was going to cower there like a scared rabbit. Unfortunately, her enormous hat tipped forward as she raised her head, and she couldn't see a damn thing. Immediately, Jack reached out and pulled it off, restoring her sight, but she wasn't grateful.

"Give me back my hat."

He looked terrible. Terrible and wonderful, in the way that only he could manage. But there was a black mood there, lurking inside his steely gray eyes, and she didn't think it was just temper directed at her. No, he was positively radiating malevolent energy, as if he'd woken up on the wrong side of the universe.

"What are you doing here?" she rasped. She ripped her hat out of his hand, nearly smacking an engrossed Sheri on the backswing.

"Coming after you," he growled. "What did you think?"

What did she think? She thought she desperately wanted to slap him with the hat that languished dangerously in her hand. She could slap him right on that beautiful, beard-shadowed jaw. Or maybe on one of those broad, gorgeous shoulders, or all the way down that long duster coat that made him look like he just stepped out of a Jesse James movie.

"You followed me, you swine. Why did you follow me?"

"Let's not play games, okay?"

"Play games?" she seethed. "Play games? Who's playing games here, me or you? Who said, and I quote, 'It's too late for ladylike gestures. Either you stay here and finish what you started, or get out of town.' That was it, wasn't it?" she challenged. In her best imitation of his gruff, rough voice, she added the finale, " 'With me, lady, there's no middle ground.' "

"So?"

"So—so you told me to get out of town, and I did. And now here you are, after me. What's the matter, change your mind? I thought with you, there was no middle ground." She couldn't understand why those words had come back to her so easily. They were eerily familiar, as a matter of fact. "Why do I know those lines?"

"Because I said them."

"No," she said with growing horror. "Because I wrote them! Holy smokes, Jack, I put those exact words in a book. But which one?" Was it possible he'd said the same thing by accident? "No way." She grabbed him by the lapels of his lousy, incredibly sexy duster. "Which one did you read, damn you?"

"All of them," he returned, detaching her hands from his coat as a bunch of curious Scarlett O'Haras and Cinderellas pushed in for a closer look.

"All of them? You read all my..." She stepped back. "But why?"

He clenched his jaw, making that stark line even harder. "I thought it might help me deal with you. Since you were pretty much running roughshod there at the beginning."

"Roughshod?"

"And then using Black Jack's strategy seemed like a good idea to get rid of you." His brows lowered. "Worked for him."

Madison felt wounded, as if she were some bull in a china shop or something. Around Jack, she wanted to feel small and feminine and clingy, like that whole crop of Scarletts hanging on his every word, with their cleavage falling out of their gowns and their cutesy curls bouncing. Instead, she felt like a fool. He'd used her own words to maneuver her out of his life.

"I can't believe you did that," she said softly. "That was very unkind."

"An even better reason to stay away from me," he said roughly. "So I guess I did you a favor, making you leave."

"A favor? Exactly." Madison backed away, but there was nowhere to go. "You're right. It was the best idea in the world for me to get out of your damn bedroom and out of that cesspool, Godforsaken."

Jack's lips tightened into a grim line. "So why in the hell did you make sure I'd come after you?"

Standing her ground, Madison gave him a level stare. It wasn't easy to maintain her dignity when she felt her gigantic pants threatening to slip down and embarrass her every time she breathed. With a fierce grip on her waistband, she said bravely, "I may have needed a bit of space, to clear my head, but I never had any intention of abandoning our caper."

"Our what?"

"Caper," she repeated, with more than a bit of annoyance. "It's a perfectly good word. It means an escapade, an adventure."

"I know what it means, but this isn't it," he said between gritted teeth.

"Of course it is." Ignoring all the eavesdroppers and interested glances they were attracting, she declared, "Diamond mines, drug lords, and all those fascinating maps to be decoded and deciphered. If this isn't a caper, I don't know what is."

"Excuse me," interrupted a beauteous young miss squeezed into an abbreviated Pebbles Flintstone getup. The girl with the bone in her hair tugged on Jack's sleeve. "Are you Black Jack Brogan? The real one, I mean? Can I have your autograph?"

"I wrote him, I created him, and you want *his* autograph?" Madison demanded, wrenching the cocktail napkin away from the dopey cave child.

"Well, yeah." Pebbles shrugged, grabbing back her napkin and sticking it up closer to Jack's face. "This place is full of writers, honey," she told Madison. "But there's only one of him."

"Don't call me honey," Madison muttered.

Jack seemed to be bemused, or at least confused, but he signed the napkin for Pebbles, after which a whole line of sirens and nymphettes queued up to get his signature. Outraged, incredulous, Madison could only watch.

"Are you going to do this all night?" she asked hotly.

"You got a better idea?"

"Yes. Tell them to go away so you and I can finish our discussion." She knocked the nearest elbow, neatly spilling fruit punch on Jack's last autograph.

"Discussion? You mean this isn't a fight?"

"No," she said brightly. "But it soon will be."

"Okay, Mad," he returned, shooing away the gaggle of girls. Edging in closer, he took Madison's arm and began to steer her through the buzzing crowd. "You've got my attention. What are you going to do with it?"

She let herself be dragged along, but she didn't like it. "Why did you come here, anyway?"

"You took what belongs to me," he whispered, breathing warm air in her ear, sending tingles down the entire length of her spine. "I want back what's mine."

"What if I don't want to give it back?"

He smiled. She could feel his lips curve, right there next to her ear. "Then I'm gonna haul your pretty little butt someplace more private and see if I can't persuade you."

Chapter Eight

Wind whipped at him, threatening to knock him off the train and down into one of the deep ravines that lined the tracks. But Black Jack flattened himself and crawled on, determined to catch the wily robber who'd eluded him for so long.

"Gotcha," he grunted, grabbing the man's boot. With a burst of strength, Black Jack flipped the robber over, ripping the bandanna from that elusive face. "Godawmighty." He sat back in surprise, almost toppling off the train. "You're a woman."

"Go to hell!" she shouted, spitting at him.

But a bullet pinged off the top of the train car, not far from Black Jack's leg. With one swift whoosh, he slammed down on top of the little spitfire, pinning her body under his own, feeling every curve press up against him.

Another bullet ricocheted, only inches away. With a wicked smile, Black Jack found her mouth with his own, kissing her hard and long. And then he vaulted over her and down the side of the train car.

Danger had never felt so good.

Black Jack Brogan, Book # 14
Jack-Knife

"I'm not going anywhere with you," Madison insisted. "Private or otherwise." But she let him keep pulling her along toward the door, at least for the time being.

"Can't take the heat?"

"Maybe I don't want to hear any more of my own books quoted back at me." She stopped dead. "Oh, my God. I finally placed it. 'Either you stay here and finish what you started, or get out of town....' *Between a Jack and a Hard Place.*" Madison felt the color drain from her face. She raised accusing eyes to Jack. "He called her Lola. And you called me Kandy. You stole the whole thing!"

Good grief. He really had no shame. None. He'd put the moves on her on purpose, just to get rid of her, and when that didn't work, he'd coldly called her by another woman's name.

Deep down, Madison felt insulted and betrayed. None of it had been real. Not even when he kissed her, or held her, or brushed his lips over the pale curve of her breast....

She closed her eyes, willing herself not to blush and make things worse. Remembering that kiss, remembering the stormy light in his eyes, the feel of his arms around her, she had to clench her teeth and think about sea slugs just to keep on an even keel. The important thing was that he'd tricked her, using her own words against her, not whatever meaningless, superficial intimacies had passed between them.

Meaningless? Superficial? Madison fiddled with her earring, a tiny top hat from a Monopoly game, while she tried not to remember the intimacies in question. They certainly hadn't felt meaningless to her at the time.

Jack just stood there, looking at her, scorching her with that hot, silvery gaze, until she felt her face flush and her toes tingle all over again. She wanted to be strong, to stand there stock-still and take whatever he dished out, but she couldn't. She had to kind of wiggle a little, tap her fingers, jiggle one foot, or the heat deep inside her would blaze out and fry her where she stood. All because Jack was looking at her that way.

"It is very upsetting for you to stand there and stare at me like I'm some kind of Martian or something," she managed.

It was devastating. And he got to her without lifting a finger. Of course, if he did lift a finger, it would be far worse, far hotter, far more fun. But she couldn't think about that. Not after what he'd done.

She almost panicked just contemplating Jack pawing through her love scenes. She expected people to read what she wrote. But Jack wasn't *people*.

Jack was...whatever it was that made ordinary men into matinee idols, that made strong women beg, that made smart women run for cover. Jack was that and more. And Madison didn't want him reading her most intimate thoughts, her dreams, her fantasies. What else was he going to come up with to ambush her with, once he'd read all her private thoughts?

Well, the best defense was a good offense. "I just realized something else," she said warily. "That quote was from *Between a Jack and a Hard Place*, which isn't even out yet. How did you read a book that hasn't been published?"

"Maybe it was ESP."

"ESP?"

He smiled, that crooked, cynical grin that took her breath away. "Maybe I just concentrated and the whole book came to me in psychic waves."

Madison crossed her arms over her bright blue tail-coat. "And maybe I'm the Queen of Sheba."

"No, I think that woman over there is the Queen of Sheba. You're the Mad Hatter, if I'm not mistaken."

"She's Delilah, you fool." She wanted to slug him. She really did. Instead, it was the best she could do to keep a good hold on her pants. "How did you get your hands on *Between a Jack and a Hard Place*? I want to know, and I want to know now."

"Connections," he said calmly. "I have connections."

"To whom?"

"That would be telling."

"Yes, it would." Madison kept her voice down only with the strictest self-control. "So come on, Jack. Tell already!"

"Excuse me," a tall man in a white rabbit suit interrupted, tapping Jack on the arm and sticking a black ice-cream cone of a microphone in his face. "Are you really Black Jack Brogan?"

The microphone was shoved in Jack's face. Adding to the equation was a man in jeans with a small TV camera slung over his shoulder, recording the whole episode.

Fluffing her bangs, Madison smiled sunnily for the camera, noting, "I think you interviewed me a few months ago, when a network was talking about a Black Jack Brogan miniseries. I'm Madison Talley, the author of the Black Jack books. Do you remember me?"

"Right," the guy said, but he quickly switched his focus back to Jack, who had turned away slightly, keeping his face partially hidden. "Are you or are you not the real Black Jack Brogan?" the reporter persisted.

"Black Jack is fictional," Madison put in helpfully. "This gentleman is *not* Black Jack. He's..."

But she suddenly realized she had no idea who he was.

"Who are you?" the guy inquired, again extending the microphone, and Madison waited with bated breath to hear the answer. "Everybody wants to know."

But Jack didn't reply. His face was even more forbidding than when he'd stalked across the ballroom to confront her, and she had the distinct feeling that he did not want to be anywhere near a television camera.

"I'm nobody, okay?" he said, spreading a hand in front of the lens.

"Come on, guy, give us a break," interrupted a different reporter, this one wearing a striped suit and a porkpie hat, right out of an old movie. "This party's a real drag. You're our only chance at a story. Are you somebody? Are you the real Black Jack Brogan?"

"I told you, there is no real Black Jack," Madison said angrily. "I made him up. Completely. All by myself."

"Oh, come on, lady. Everybody here thinks this is the guy." The second reporter elbowed her out of the way, shoving a mini-tape recorder practically up Jack's nose. "It's a great story if there's a real guy behind the character. Stranger than fiction, and nobody knew. Good angle."

"You are Black Jack, aren't you?" the guy asked again. "I heard her call you Jack. And she based the books on you, right?"

"I'm sure you find it reassuring to believe there has to be a man at the center of every success story." With determination, Madison placed herself back inside the interrogation circle. "But as I've been trying to tell you, I made up Black Jack myself. Without any help from anyone with testosterone!"

"No, Madison," Jack said kindly, laying a hand on her arm and tugging her back closer to him, as if she were under his protection. "It's no use. We might as well tell them the truth."

"The truth?" she echoed, staring up at him aghast. She'd never heard Jack use that namby-pamby tone, as if he were chagrined, a tad sheepish.

"Yes, the truth."

He tightened his hold on her, squeezing her gently, still acting twinkly and avuncular. She'd never seen this quick a personality change—it was like Dr. Jekyll and Mr. Hyde. On the whole, she preferred the other, surlier personality. What was he up to?

"You're right," he announced to the reporters, as Madison gasped. "I am Black Jack Brogan. The real one."

She tried to head him off, to deny it, but he squeezed her harder, and she could hardly breathe, let alone refute his crazy statements. Besides, no one was listening to her anyway, not with a fake Black Jack Brogan tossing out true confessions.

"I met Madison years ago, before she wrote her first book under her own name, back when she was still one of the stable of writers who did the Rod... ooph—"

Panicking, Madison elbowed him in the ribs and cut him off, before he could do the unthinkable and remind the whole world that she'd been a Roderick Tweed hack. "I don't think we should talk about this," she warned.

"She's shy," he said sweetly, holding her tightly. By now, the original two members of the press had been joined by their colleagues, creating a little cluster of newshounds all around Jack. It was like they smelled a story in the making at the otherwise sedate Literary Ball, and nobody wanted to miss out.

Meanwhile, Madison was stunned. Shy? Her? Who was he kidding? And why was he going forward with this, pretending to be Black Jack? Surely he'd expose it as a joke within the next three seconds. And what if he didn't? What was she going to say?

Showing every indication of continuing the farce, Jack dropped a kiss on the top of her head. Madison steamed, but what could she do? Without knowing his real name, she could hardly expose him. All she knew were Cutter, Ballantine and MacChesney, who still sounded outrageously familiar.

And then she got a funny feeling. *"Gunga Din,"* she said suddenly.

Everybody looked at her all at once. *"Gunga Din?"* the rabbit reporter asked. "What do you mean, *Gunga Din*?"

"Nothing. She doesn't mean anything." Jack framed her face with his hands, giving her a quick kiss to shut her up, ordering, "Let me tell the story, will you, darling?"

"I remember," she whispered, struggling away from his damn lying lips. "Cutter, MacChesney and Ballantine—they're the characters in *Gunga Din.*"

But Jack shoved her halfway behind him as he improvised some half-witted story about how he and Madison had met at a revival movie house playing *Gunga Din.* "We saw each other there for the fourth time, watching the same movie, and we knew it was fated to be."

"Oh, Jack," she groaned. "That's terrible. Why did you tell them that?"

"Don't be embarrassed," the reporter chided her. "It's very sweet, very romantic. Your fans will love it. Bestselling novelist gets her inspiration from a real-life hero she met at the movies. What could be more romantic?"

Madison knew she had to stop this before Jack made up even more convoluted lies. *Gunga Din,* indeed. Why would he adopt names from an old, creaky movie nobody but her was screwy enough to remember anyway? But then, why did he do anything?

"Jack," she said meaningfully, leaning in close enough to deliver her message right into his ear. "Either you stop this right now, or I'm screaming at the top of my lungs that you're a fraud and a thief."

He turned his head and sent her a cynical smile. "What a good idea, Mad," he murmured under his breath, so only she could hear. "You tell them I'm a thief, and I'll spill everything I know about you. You know, Mad, all that good stuff about the private papers you lifted from my hotel room, after you broke in and vandalized the place."

"Vandalized? A few cookie crumbs, and you call it vandalized?"

"Yes, I do," he said calmly. "I can see the headlines: Bestselling author accused of breaking and entering, burglary, criminal trespass, destruction of property. Good stuff for TV and the magazines."

"You . . . ?" But it didn't matter. He was right. After all, she *had* gotten in under false pretenses, and she had stolen a few insignificant items. One quick look at the camera crew and the collection of print reporters, holding their notebooks at the ready, convinced her it was a good idea to keep her mouth shut.

"You got me into this, honey bun," he said, smiling again in that nasty way he did so well. "I thought I might as well have some fun." And then he hauled her up against him, kissing her soundly, providing a touching photo opportunity for the press.

"Two lovebirds," the reporter groused. "So tell us, Black Jack, how much input do you have in the books? You're the role model, right? Anything more to it than that?"

Setting a shaken Madison back down on her feet, Jack grinned modestly. "As a matter of fact, there's a lot more to it. At the beginning, I was just the jumping-off point. Madison's inspiration, you might say, her ideal hero, the man of her dreams."

"I know what I'd like to see jumping off," she muttered. "You, off a bridge. Or maybe the Empire State Building."

"But as we went along," he continued, riding roughshod over her words, "I got more involved. She'd always borrowed events from my real life and used them for the books, after adapting them to the nineteenth century, of course."

"Of course," they all murmured, as if they'd all read the books, which she would've bet her last dollar they hadn't.

"Borrowing events from your real life?" This was a nightmare. She would've said it was her worst nightmare, but then she recalled slugging back tequila and passing out on Jack's bed. She remembered lying on the bed with him, getting aroused and steamy, before he'd called her Kandy. Now *that* was awful. This was only irritating and humiliating.

"And now," Jack said, with charm positively dripping from his traitor's voice. "Now I'm really participating. I'm actually writing—"

"Writing?" Madison gave him a swift kick in the ankle. "Oh, no, you don't! This is going too far."

"Madison!" Sheri cried, her eyes round with surprise. She and Marley had apparently been hanging around the fringe of the impromptu press conference, and now Sheri tapped her on the shoulder, clearly shocked by Jack's announcement. "I never knew there was a real Black Jack behind your books. I didn't even know you had a boyfriend. How did you keep him a secret all this time?"

"He writes your books?" demanded Marley, looking like a very gleeful ghost all of a sudden. "The cowboy writes your books? Little Madison, pretending to be the writer, when she's fronting for—"

"I write my own books!"

"Of course she does." Jack grinned for the crowd, flashing a real showstopper of a smile. "I just help a little."

"A little?" If any more steam had come out of her ears, she would've whistled like a teakettle. "Jack, how dare you say these things?"

"Madison, is this true?" Sheri asked.

"I love it!" Marley said, rubbing his hands together.

"Did you get that?" the TV reporter asked his cameraman. "Great. Thanks, everyone."

"Black Jack, I have a couple more questions," somebody called out, and Jack looked completely capable of spinning lies all night.

"No," Madison said distinctly. "No more of this."

"But—" they all chorused.

"No!" Madison repeated, in her deadliest voice. "No more questions."

"I guess that's all, folks," Jack told them.

The reporters fell back in the face of Madison's fury and Jack's taciturn smile. Grabbing his hand, she decided to get out while the getting was good. She wrenched him away from the cacophony, dragging his impossible hide through a sea of interested bystanders and up the elevator to her room before he could say another word.

"That was so low," she told him for the forty-fifth time, as she slid the key in the door of her penthouse suite. "Pond scum isn't that low."

"Nice digs," he said casually, glancing around at the posh suite.

"Harvey arranged it. My agent." When she'd checked in, she'd thought it was a cool and restful place, all done in peaches and creams, with two bedrooms, a separate living room, and even a romantic balcony with a spectacular view of the Seattle skyline. Now, however, it did not feel restful in the least. "Don't think you're going to get me off the subject by complimenting my accommodations. I'm still furious that you made up all that garbage. Furious!'' she emphasized.

''You could always have told them the truth.''

''Oh, right. And risk looking like a fool on national television?''

She stomped into the living room and dumped her hat and her Mad Hatter tailcoat onto the soft peach sofa. Even though the sliding door to the balcony was open, letting in a lovely evening breeze, it suddenly felt very hot and stuffy in the suite.

''It's just that I'm wearing so many clothes,'' she muttered under her breath, and she stripped off her striped vest and her bow tie, adding them to the pile of discarded clothing. ''It couldn't possibly be that he's in my room, getting me all hot and bothered, and that's why my temperature keeps rising. Don't even think it, Madison. It's just hot. It's not him.''

''What are you mumbling about?''

''Not a thing.''

But she realized with a rush of apprehension exactly what it meant that Jack was here, in her suite. She'd given him what he'd wanted when he first found her in the ballroom, namely a place to be alone, a place where she was completely at his mercy.

I'm gonna haul your pretty little butt someplace more private, and see if I can't persuade you, he'd said.

I'm not going anywhere with you, private or otherwise, she'd retorted. And yet here she was, in his clutches. What was he planning to do, anyway? Madison shivered. Damn the man. He always got what he wanted, and she was always left wanting.

The fabric of her vest was shot through with silver threads, the same electric shade as Jack's eyes. It was infuriating that everything she looked at reminded her of him and his nefarious charm. The vest was the last straw. So she sat on it. But she was too angry to sit down for long.

"How dare you, Jack?"

He shrugged, still lounging in the open doorway. "What was I supposed to do? As long as everybody already thought I was Black Jack, it seemed like a convenient identity to use for a while."

"Jack, you don't seem to understand. You told all those people you write my books." Grabbing his lapels, she yanked him into the room and slammed the door behind him. And then she advanced on him, poking him in the chest with one finger. "My books are sacred, sacrosanct, off-limits, taboo. Nobody and nothing touches my books."

"Aren't you being a little overdramatic?"

She took him by the shoulders and shook him. "Overdramatic? Are you crazy?" He was solid as the Rock of Gibraltar and she didn't shake him much, but she felt like she got her point across.

She also felt like she'd been stung, just from touching him for a second and a half. Her hands dropped to her sides and she jammed them into the pockets of her baggy checked pants. She didn't want to fight with him; she wanted to pick up where they'd left off in that terrible motel room in Godforsaken. In lieu of that, she supposed fighting with him was the next best thing.

She finished hotly, "I'm not the one who told people we met at *Gunga Din. Gunga Din,* for goodness' sake. What's the big deal about *Gunga Din,* anyway?"

"I like *Gunga Din.*"

"I'll remember that next time I'm choosing identities."

"Come on, Mad, don't hold a grudge." He tapped her gently, knocking her back onto the couch.

From her vulnerable position, with Jack standing right in front of her, leaving her eyes at crotch level, she had to take a deep breath. Warily, she asked, "So what are you doing this time, trying to make me so mad I'll kiss our caper goodbye?" She sat up. "Because I'm not, Jack. Diamond mines, drug lords, the whole shot. I'm in."

"I know." He expelled a long breath. "Believe me, I know."

Feathering her bangs through her fingers, she glanced up at him. "So we're agreed?"

"We're not agreed on anything that I can see." He climbed over her, knocking the haphazard array of her clothes onto the floor with one hand. And then he stretched out his long legs next to hers on the couch.

She sat up straighter. "What are you doing?"

"Relaxing. I've had a hard couple of days."

"You did? Why?"

"Well, Mad, after I figured out that you'd taken off with half my files, I decided to come after you." His lips narrowed into a mocking smile. "But somebody had other ideas."

"What do you mean?"

"Somebody hit me over the head." He leaned back into the fat cushions of the lush peach sofa. "I woke up facedown in the dirt about five hours later, with a headache like you wouldn't believe. So you'll excuse me if I'm not my usual perky self."

"Perky? You? Don't make me laugh." Madison scooted over closer, trying to see if there was a bump or any other wound on his head without actually touching him. "Oh, the heck with it," she grumbled, gingerly probing his soft black hair. "Are you hurt? You could have a concussion, you know."

"Madison, I don't think you should do that," he said softly.

But his hair was so soft, and her fingers kept gently massaging the back of his head. "Do what?" she asked innocently, rubbing her fingers against his head to a rhythm she felt echo deep inside.

"You're driving me crazy."

What a delicious thought. "Am I—?" But that was all she had time to get out.

Without warning, Jack flipped her over, back into the couch cushions, covering her body with his longer, harder frame. "Madison," he whispered. "Please be quiet."

"Yes," she whispered back, tangling her arms around him, pushing that damn duster off his shoulders, pulling him down to her eager mouth. She was on fire. All the passion she'd been suppressing while she argued with him came roaring to the top, brimming over, licking her with hot flames.

Her too-big pants had gotten scrunched up and rolled down at the waist when she fell back with Jack, and they'd left about a three-inch gap as they pooled around her hips. "Oh, hellfire," she muttered, maneuvering herself around enough to kick the troublesome pants off and out of her way.

"Madison," he breathed in her ear, "I wanted to take this slow. And I'm perfectly capable of getting rid of your clothes myself." He bit her ear, ignoring the tiny top hat. "Slowly." He licked her ear. "Very slowly."

"Oh, my..." The air was getting thinner on this couch, and her heartbeat had accelerated past what was safe. "My pants kept falling off," she murmured, wondering why in the world she was bothering to answer. But her brain seemed to have disengaged itself while she wasn't paying attention, and she could only let her tongue run on, unimpeded. Sliding one bare leg up and down the worn, faded fabric of his blue jeans, she said, sighing, "Besides, this is nice."

"Very nice."

Jack's hands slipped to the collar of her shirt and he ripped it open with one decisive slash, popping buttons every which way. The savage sound inflamed her even more, as cool air rushed over her fevered skin. Her nipples hardened under the silk chemise she'd worn beneath her costume, and the feel of silk and desire wound together with everything Jack was doing. It was intoxicating.

"Yours, too," she demanded, ripping his black cotton shirt off with the same ferocious need. His chest was wonderful, taut and muscular, with just a light covering of dark hair. His hair felt soft against the hardness of his chest and she rubbed her breasts across it, delighting in his low moan of response.

His hands cupped her bottom through the silk chemise, and Madison returned the favor, sidling up against him and those wonderful tight jeans even closer, lifting herself into his embrace.

The image of what he undoubtedly wore under those jeans popped into her mind. She couldn't help but think of all those skimpy little black briefs she'd fingered in his drawers and what they'd look like stretched across Jack's tight, hard body. She swallowed, but her fingers were already sneaking to the snap at the top of his jeans. The slight pop echoed in her brain, but she pressed on, pushing the jeans away, dying to open this lovely male package and see what was inside.

Just as Madison reached for him, fingering the waistband of his racy black briefs, the glass vase on the coffee table in front of them exploded.

And then the coffee table itself exploded. Madison lifted her head, unable to make sense of any of it, but Jack shoved her back into the sofa fiercely, hiding her underneath his long, strong body.

"Don't move," he said tersely, pulling his jeans back on. "Somebody's shooting at us."

Chapter Nine

Black Jack awoke when the cold water hit his crotch.

"What the . . . ?" His mouth fell open as he sat up in the ornate old bed. "Princess Alexandra, is that you?"

"Of course," she said cheerfully, stripping off the dreary guise of an upstairs maid.

"Why are you dressed like that?"

But the pretty little princess was already hopping into bed beside him. "I had to see you somehow, didn't I?"

He grabbed the driest part of the bed linens, gamely trying to cover his nakedness. "I don't know what to say."

"Hello might be nice." And then she was wiggling her soft body all over his.

Could he be hanged for doing this with a crown princess? Could he be hanged for not doing it?

"Hello, Alexandra," he said softly. He began to kiss her back.

Black Jack Brogan, Book #9
Jack Jump Over the Candlestick

"Shooting at us?" Madison tried to push her way out from under him, but he wouldn't budge. "What in the world are you talking about? People don't shoot at people like me. I write books!"

But something whizzed past their heads, sailing over the back of the couch, impacting the wall near the front door, scarring the wallpaper and puffing plaster into the air from a nice round hole.

"Somebody is definitely shooting. Walls don't put holes in themselves. And I don't see any other targets handy, do you?" he asked cynically. "It's either you or me. Or maybe both of us."

"But why?"

"Got me." He arched a dark eyebrow. "There've been several times when I wanted to kill you. Maybe somebody else had the same idea. You been plaguing anybody else lately, or it is just me?"

"That's a really nasty thing to say."

But it was hard to hold a grudge when his warm, hard body was still pressing her into the couch, when she could feel the imprint of the open button at the top of his jeans, biting into her stomach, and the heady sanctuary of his arms, so close around her. She tried to edge to the side, to move just enough to not feel all these dangerous emotions, but it was impossible. Even with people shooting and vases blowing up right before her eyes, all she wanted was to get rid of Jack's clothes and bite him somewhere wicked.

"Quit wiggling," he said in an ominous tone. "We're both a lot safer if you just hold still."

"How can I hold still?" she whispered fiercely. "I may die any minute and I never got to make lo..." *Oh, dear.* What was she thinking of, saying that to him? She tried again. "I never got to feel what it would be like if you touched..." *Worse.* "What I mean is, it seems wrong that you and I, that *we,* never experienced..." *The worst.* Her whole body suffused with hot color and she clamped her mouth shut.

"You better shut up while you're ahead, Mad." Jack kissed her quickly, savagely. "But hold that thought."

Silently, he eased off her, over the side of the sofa, till he was crouching on the floor.

"Where are you going?" she whispered.

Two more shots reported, this time blowing holes in the carpet next to the sofa, filling the air with the smell of burnt wool. Madison flinched, but she repeated her urgent question.

"Where are you going?"

"Be quiet, Madison," he whispered back. "I know that's tough for you, but keep it zipped, okay?"

"Where are you going?"

He sighed. "I'm trying to figure out where the shots are coming from. Is that a balcony over there?"

"Yes." In fact, she could still feel cool air blowing faintly into the room through the open door. As Jack crawled away, angling for a better view of their assailant, Madison reached out and hooked him by the waist of his jeans. "Psst, Jack."

"I ought to have my head examined," he growled. But he turned back. "What, Madison? What is it?"

"The balcony," she told him. "The door was open when we came in. I don't think I left it open."

"So somebody's been hiding out there ever since we got here. Either we caught this guy mid-burglary, or he was waiting to ambush us."

"I—I guess so." She pulled him back far enough to wrap her arms around his bare chest, to give him a swift, frantic kiss on the lips. "I'm sorry about your head. And I'm sorry about the shooting. But I'm really glad you were here, Jack, that I didn't come back here alone."

"Yeah, me, too." He detached her arms gently. "Now I want you to just sit here and be quiet. Let me handle it."

"I'm not scared," she bluffed. "This is exciting. I've never been shot at before."

"Yeah, I know." He glanced at her, shook his head, and then curved his narrow lips into a bemused smile. "You're one of a kind, Mad."

"I hope I stay one of a kind. I hope I stay *anything.*"

He fingered her cheek. "I'm sure whoever it is just wants out of here. There's nothing to worry about." But he pulled her back for one last embrace, holding her close as he whispered, "It's going to be okay. I can take care of it, Mad. I can take care of you. And when we're out of this, I'm going to come back and make love to you for a long, long time. That's a promise you can count on."

She dropped her head to his shoulder, breathing in the smell of sweat, desire and Jack. All Jack. She was scared to death he'd do what he'd promised, and scared to death he wouldn't. *A promise she could count on...* She couldn't have written better dialogue for Jack if she'd tried. She sincerely hoped she hadn't, that this time he wasn't just stealing lines from one of her books.

"I don't care if I did write it," she muttered. "It still sounds good to me."

"You didn't write it." Jack smoothed the short wisps of her hair back from her face, brushing his thumbs down her cheekbones as he stared straight into her eyes, giving her the full benefit of that steady, steely gaze. "Stay here, all right?"

She nodded, making herself very small and squishing herself down into the couch cushions. She watched Jack inch out around the couch, just enough to peek in the direction of the balcony. But another blast knocked him back.

"Definitely the balcony," he said grimly. And then he took Madison's white tuxedo shirt, the one she'd worn with her Mad Hatter costume, waving it in the air above their heads. "Hey, you," he shouted. "What do you want?"

But the only answer was the rat-a-tat of an automatic weapon, shooting holes in the shirt.

"I think he wants us," Madison said, trembling so hard she could barely speak. The sight of her very own blouse full of bullet holes was a pretty chilly dose of reality. "Dead."

A spray of shots followed, as if the gunman had gone bonkers at the last minute, using up every piece of ammo he had in a blaze of glory. Without hesitating, Jack threw himself over Madison, knocking the wind out of her. She recovered enough to cover his head with a couch cushion as they both burrowed deep into the poor, much abused sofa. The rain of bullets continued, pinging as it contacted wood, muffled as it hit stuffing and fabric, but destroying everything it touched.

Boom. Down went the lamp and the room pitched into partial darkness, lit only by the skyline of Seattle, twinkling out there beyond the balcony.

In all the din, Madison could barely make out the sound of feet, running from the balcony to the door, as the barrage of shots moved with the gunman. It felt like forever, as she huddled under Jack, not really giving herself time to be scared. She was with Jack, wasn't she? Everything would be okay.

And then, after one last burst of bullets, the room went very still. No more shots, no more breaking glass, no more anything. Except Jack, breathing steadily above her, his chest rising and falling rhythmically, smack up against her breasts.

She had forgotten to breathe. It would've been impossible, anyway, wedged under a hundred and eighty pounds of sinew and muscle, but she should at least have tried to breathe. Maybe then she wouldn't be lying here, dizzy and perspiring, gulping for air.

Standing abruptly, Jack batted her protective cushion away, offering a hand to pull her to her feet. He gave her a quick once-over, as if checking for bullet holes. "Are you okay?"

"Yes. Oh, yes." She gazed up at her knight in shining armor. "Jack, you threw your body over mine, shielding me from the gunfire! You're so heroic. I knew you would be, but you've surpassed even my standards, which, you have to admit, are pretty high."

"Oh, God." Jack sank back onto the couch, burying his head in his hands.

"But, Jack, why didn't you go after him?"

Madison edged carefully around and through the destruction, wrenching open the door into the corridor, paying no attention to the fact that she was wearing only a thin slip.

"No, there's no sign of him," she announced. "Too bad. You missed him, Jack."

"Missed him?" Following her, he yanked her back out of the doorway and slammed the thing shut. "Who do you think I am, the Terminator? That guy had a gun. Automatic weapons, Mad. What have I got? One crazy woman and half a broken lamp? What do you want me to do, force his fingers into a socket and electrocute him?"

"Oh." Her euphoria faded quickly. Madison stepped over a pile of broken glass left behind from the destruction of the coffee table. "I guess I wasn't thinking."

"I guess you weren't," he said gruffly.

"I already said you were heroic," she tried. "Just because you didn't run after him doesn't mean you weren't already being brave and heroic and wonderful."

"Gee, thanks, Mad." With a dark frown, Jack picked up and put down the ruined lampshade. "Well, I guess we're going to have to figure out who did this, and why."

We. He'd said *we* were going to figure it out. Madison smiled with delight. He'd finally gotten used to having her around, to the idea that this was a partnership. And she hadn't forgotten how tender and sweet he'd acted for a few minutes there, when he'd touched her hair and told her he'd protect her.

He'd also told her he'd make love to her. For a long, long time.

She shivered. If only she could get back that moment, recreate the steamy, sexy look in his eyes, and start all over. But it was too late now. Now that she'd done whatever it was she'd done to annoy him this time. He was the jumpiest, most changeable man she'd ever met.

"Are you cold?" he asked, tossing her the bright blue tailcoat she'd worn as the Mad Hatter.

She caught it, but made no move to put it on. "Cold? No, not at all. You could, uh, shut the balcony door if you're cold, though."

"I'm not cold. I just think you should be wearing something."

She hadn't realized how skimpy her chemise was until she glanced down at it. Once again, she felt a blush sweep her from head to foot, and the hot color only served to outline the dark circles of her nipples, hardening as they peeked through the thin silk of her slip. She crossed her arms over her chest immediately, murmuring something about a robe as she ducked into the bedroom of the suite.

She was just belting a big chenille robe, the thickest thing she owned, as she ventured back into the chaos of the living room. Jack was over by the balcony, fiddling with the lock on the door, and then he crouched down to check out every inch of the balcony itself just as thoroughly.

"Yeah, somebody was standing here for a while. It must've rained earlier, and it was dirty on the balcony. The mud's pretty thin, but you can see a footprint. Small guy, though. Maybe a woman."

"There's one good thing," Madison offered.

He glanced up. "What's that?"

"Well, at least the person wasn't trying to kill us. That's good news."

Jack rose to his feet slowly. "Why do you think that?"

"Look at this place, Jack." She waved a hand at the destruction. "If he—or she—had wanted to kill us, it wouldn't have taken this many bullets to do it. We were just lying there, like lambs at the slaughter, and all he had to do was point. To use this many bullets and *not* hit us, he had to be trying pretty hard."

There was a pause as Jack seemed to mull over her deduction. She figured he'd disagree with her, just on principle. But finally, reluctantly, he said, "Good point. I think you're right."

"So if he didn't want to murder us, what was he doing here?"

"Burglary?" Jack asked quietly. "We interrupted him while he was stealing something, and he holed up on the balcony hoping to wait us out. But then we started getting cozy on the couch."

"Getting, uh, cozy. Right." His face looked stern, but Madison felt her own cheeks bloom yet again with color. "He figured we weren't going to leave, and he was stranded."

"Exactly," Jack returned. "And so he shot his way out of here."

Madison shook her head. "Very sloppy. Very, very sloppy."

"So he's a stupid burglar."

"An amateur. Yes, I suppose that fits."

"Or maybe he was just jealous." A tiny flicker of amusement lit Jack's eyes. "Hasn't had a woman in a long time."

Madison licked her lips. "And how does that, uh, figure in?" she asked in a husky voice she had trouble controlling.

"We were..."

"Getting cozy," she supplied.

"Getting cozy. Right in front of him." Hands stuck in the pockets of his jeans, Jack strolled over a little closer. "Couldn't take the heat. Blasted things up before we had a chance to take it any further."

"Oh, that's good," Madison whispered. "That's very good."

He leaned over her, lowering his head, and Madison felt herself stretching up to meet his caress. His hands were still in his pockets, and no piece of him was actually touching her. He just hovered there, and she waited, tantalized, scandalized, hypnotized.

"Oh, Jack," she breathed.

"Madison," he whispered. "Hold still."

"Yes."

His lips drifted from one corner of her mouth to the other, not making contact, just threatening. "What was our burglar after?"

Her eyes fluttered closed, and she tilted up even closer. "I—I don't know."

"I think I do." His lips brushed her cheek and her ear. "I think I know exactly what he wanted."

"What?" she murmured.

"My papers." His voice hardened as he took her shoulders in his hands. "The things you stole from me. Where are they?"

"Your papers?" And then it became clear. "Oh, my God." She almost slapped him, but held her hand back just in time. "All of this—all of this 'let's go somewhere private' routine—it was just another trick, a trick to get me up here so you could steal back your stupid papers!"

"Since they were mine in the first place, I don't call it stealing."

"I do," she said hotly. She wrenched herself out of his grasp. "I keep forgetting how low you can go."

"Me? You're the one who ripped me off and then was careless enough to let the stuff get stolen right out from under your nose."

"Oh, pooh." She crossed her arms over her chest. "I was hardly careless—I mean, you had them lying around like goods at a fire sale—and besides, we don't yet know that they're missing, and how would anyone know I had them in the first place?"

"Maybe they followed me to you."

"Followed you to... You don't really think...?"

Spinning away, Madison raced into the bedroom, her chenille robe swirling around her, with Jack not far behind. Quickly, she tossed a large suitcase onto the bed and tore it open, shoving aside lingerie and rumpled clothing. She pried up the bottom lining of the case, but there was nothing there. "I had it in a file folder," she said softly. "I put it under the lining. It's gone."

"Well, that answers that."

Jack's voice was bleak, and she hastened to reassure him. "It's not so terrible, really it isn't. I made copies."

His head snapped her way. "Copies?"

"Not of everything, unfortunately, but all the stuff that fit on the photocopy machine. Not that big map, or any of the memos in blue ink, because they didn't reproduce very well. But everything else, I think. And the whole set of copies is here," she said triumphantly, pulling a fat file out of the back of a three-ring binder. "I hid it with the notes for my new book. You know, hide it in plain sight. Obviously that worked better than the ones I hid in a real hiding place."

"When did you get an idea for a new book?"

She found it difficult to believe he was more interested in her new book than the missing papers and the burglar and the rest of this mess. "Well, not an idea really," she hedged. "It's still in the notes-and-inspiration stage, you know, scribbles and things."

"It's not about me, is it?" he asked uneasily.

"They're all about you, Jack."

He swore under his breath, something very lively, and she had to concentrate to catch it. She wished she had a pencil handy, so she could've written it down. It was the perfect sort of vocabulary for Black Jack.

"Madison, quit looking at me like that," he snapped. "You can't write a book based on this caper, because there isn't any caper."

"If there's no caper, then why did someone go to all the trouble of committing burglary and attempted murder to get his hands on your files?"

"Don't remind me." His gaze narrowed as he grimaced in her direction. "It really burns me to know that some crackpot has copies of all my papers. Right now, he's probably slobbering all over them."

"Well, it isn't my fault," she protested.

"You stole them. If you hadn't, he couldn't have taken them from you."

"So he would've lifted them from you after he bonked you on the head in Godforsaken." Madison pulled herself together, offering Jack a pointed glare. "I should be the one who's mad, you know, since you led the bad guys right to me, and now I'm in danger, too, because of you and your dumb diamond mines."

Jack's jaw clenched in a murderous line, and she added, "Not that I'm blaming you. I wanted to be in on the caper. I knew that might mean a certain amount of risk. But still, you didn't have to bring these criminals here to my room to shoot at me."

"I'm aware of that, Madison." His voice was so low and so dangerous, it made shivers go up her spine. It was like hearing a Beretta speak. "And that's exactly why you are no longer in on this deal."

"You don't have a choice, Jack. I'm in."

"Oh, no, you're not." He snatched up the file of documents and backed up toward the living room. "Now that I have the copies," he warned her, "you're going back to being Madison Talley, girl author, and that's it."

"I am not." She flung off her robe, daring him to look at her in her slip, as she grabbed a sweatshirt and a pair of jeans out of her drawer. "Wherever you're going, I'm going. That's our deal."

Wearing a black look, he pretended to be completely absorbed in cataloging the contents of the file, and she loved the feeling of power it gave her. Maybe if she hung around in no clothes all the time, she could get him to do what she wanted. She doubted it. Her less than abundant charms would hardly keep him enticed for long.

"I intend to keep our deal," she insisted.

"You still haven't paid me."

"Oh, quit being such a baby about your money. You wouldn't let me write you a check."

"Madison, put some clothes on." He sent her a look with such malevolent power she hopped into her jeans rather than stand there and get scorched some more.

"Happy?" she asked, shrugging into the sweatshirt, pulling a faded line drawing of William Shakespeare down over her chest. "You could put a shirt on yourself, you know, if we're going to get hung up on this lack-of-clothes thing."

But she sighed with disappointment when he did. He had such a gorgeous chest, all muscle and strength, and she could've looked at it all day. Not without drooling, of course, but what was a little saliva between friends?

"Don't think you're getting around me." He slashed the last button through its hole and then started slamming his shirt into the top of his pants. "This has gotten way too dangerous for you."

"So it's '*sayonara,* sweetheart' time, huh?"

His gaze raked her. "What?"

"*Hasta la vista,* baby. Goodbye, Madison. Because you think I can't take it." She faced him off, toe to toe. "I didn't mind getting shot at in there. Well, I minded, but I didn't... I wasn't scared, okay?"

"I was," he said roughly. "I was scared like hell. Scared that you were going to die and it would be my fault."

"Oh." She swallowed. The look on his face hit her where it hurt. Could he really be that concerned for her safety? Could he really care? Tenderness bloomed inside her. "That's really sweet, Jack," she said with a shy smile.

But then common sense got the better of her. She added, "If you mean it, which of course I have no way of knowing because you are the most deceptive, manipulative man I have ever met. But if you really do mean it, it's very sweet. It's also totally unnecessary."

He expelled a harsh breath. "Hell, Mad, I never have a clue what you're trying to say."

"I'm not bailing out now, just when things are getting interesting," she said stubbornly. "You're the one who got smacked on the head and shot at. Somebody is out to get you, not me."

Jack ran an impatient hand through his hair. "Yeah, they're not out to get you. You're just nuts enough to throw yourself in the line of fire."

"Somebody has to protect you," she said brightly, patting him on one of his lovely biceps as she waltzed past him into the main room. "Hmm," she mused. She stooped to retrieve a shard of glass. "I guess we better call housekeeping or hotel security or something."

"Madison," he said, catching her from behind, pulling her closer. "This isn't a joke. And it isn't a caper. It's ugly and it's dangerous. You're out, and that's it."

But Madison had no intention of giving in on this one. "You need me," she insisted. "And I refuse to just roll over and play dead. You picked the wrong partner if that's what you want."

"Picked? Who picked who here?"

"Okay, so I picked you." She lifted her chin. "But you do need me, you know."

"No," he said flatly.

"Yes," she snapped right back.

Jack slung his long duster coat over one hand, briefly checking on the file folder he'd stuffed into the pocket. "I'm gone. You're history."

"I'm sticking with you." She grabbed the bottom end of his coat, threatening to pull him into a tug-of-war if necessary. "You know, Jack, if you won't let me come along, I'll just follow you." She got a better grip on the duster, moving in a few steps. "I'll be really clumsy and obvious—"

"Like when you followed me with Kandy?"

"No," she told him. "I tailed you just fine that time and you know it. I plan to be much worse in the future."

"Worse?"

"Much worse." She smiled with satisfaction. "I'll be horrible. I'll be insufferable. Until you give up."

Jack stood there, hanging on to his end of the coat with an iron grip, glowering at her, but Madison only widened her smile, adding all the sparkle and enthusiasm she could muster. If this was a showdown, she knew she could outlast him.

"Are you going to give up, Jack?" she taunted. But he didn't.

Finally, when her arm was throbbing from keeping the death grip on his duster, and her mouth ached from maintaining that murderous smile, finally Jack surrendered. He dropped the coat, sending her reeling backward until she regained her balance.

Triumphantly, she steadied herself. "You're giving up, aren't you?"

"I already gave up," he muttered, gritting his teeth. "You're making me as crazy as you are, standing here fighting over a damn coat I never liked all that much to begin with. You're certifiable, Madison, absolutely baying at the moon, out of your ever-loving mind. But if you want to come along, I guess I don't have any choice."

She laughed out loud and threw herself at him, proclaiming, "You won't regret this."

Too bad she already did. All the longings, all the hot, pulsating desire, came back in a flash, the minute she touched him. Her head spinning, Madison backed away, playing with a thread hanging from her sleeve. She couldn't put herself through this again and again, not when she couldn't tell if he was telling the truth or still spinning lies for her benefit.

"So now what?" she asked softly.

Jack glanced around the room with a grim expression. "I don't know about you, but I'm sick to death of the scenery in here. I say we call somebody to come and clean this up, and we get out of here. Maybe go get something to eat." His gaze swept her. "I'm starved."

She caught her breath. "Me, too."

"We finally agree on something." A spark of mischief lit his eyes. "Will wonders never cease?"

A small smile curved Madison's lips. Dinner out with Jack, like a date, like normal people. She liked the sound of that.

"Ready," she said, grabbing her huge satchel of a purse and heading for the door.

But Jack headed her off, holding her back while he took a long gander down the hallway. "Looks okay," he said finally. "Nobody out there but a maid."

"A maid?" Madison peeked out into the corridor. "Why should anyone need a maid at this hour?"

As she stuck her head out for a look, she spied a woman at the end of the corridor, dressed crisply in a white maid's uniform, mostly obscured behind a big laundry cart. As Madison watched, the woman glanced up. Their gazes locked.

"Kandy," Madison whispered.

The maid began to wrestle her cart down the long corridor, making for the elevator on the double.

"Kandy?" Jack echoed behind her. "What do you mean?"

"Kandy," she said again. She turned back to him, grabbing his shirt. "Wearing a maid's uniform!"

Chapter Ten

The stagecoach rattled along, spinning up dust in its wake. It was hotter than blazes inside.

Black Jack loosened his collar, hitching a leg up on the other seat, wedging Nell against the door. Daintily, she put her handkerchief to her nose, but it was no use. She was as hot as he was. Hotter. She fanned her flushed face, watching him hungrily.

The stage took a jolt, vaulting Nell across the seat, landing her smack-dab in Black Jack's lap. Without a word she fastened her mouth on his and he began divesting her of her damnable clothes.

And the temperature rose even higher.

Black Jack Brogan, Book #2
Jack's Wild

"You're sure it was her?"

"Of course I'm sure. She looked right at me. I couldn't miss that shifty look in her eyes, or those enormous . . ." Madison broke off. There was a time when Jack had seemed a bit too interested in certain portions of Kandy's anatomy to make Madison entirely happy, and she decided it was smarter not to tempt fate by reminding him. "Let's just say Kandy is conspicuous."

Jack dashed down the hallway, Madison at his heels, but it was too late. There was no sign of the mystery maid, although her cart had left long grooves in the carpet in front of the elevators.

"Quick," he commanded. "Maybe we can head her off with the stairs."

"Over there," Madison told him. She'd seen the door marked STAIRS when she used the ice machine next to it earlier in the evening. They both raced for the door, with Madison there a step or two ahead.

The door was heavy, made of metal, painted to blend in with the posh surroundings. Madison clasped both hands around the shiny doorknob, giving a mighty tug, but there was no give at all. The handle wouldn't turn and the door wouldn't budge.

"It's locked," she told him, but Jack took a try, too. His jaw clenched as he wrenched at the door, but there was no hope for it. "Great," Madison grumbled. "The fire exit is locked. This place goes up, and we're all toast, screaming in the hallway. *Towering Inferno*, in the flesh."

"We've got more important things to worry about at the moment," Jack noted darkly. "Like what the hell Kandy was doing here, thousands of miles from home."

"That seems pretty obvious to me, Jack." Madison leaned back against the door. "Kandy is our gunman."

"You've got to be kidding."

She crossed her arms over her William Shakespeare sweatshirt, fixing him with a placid stare. "It's the most gigantic coincidence in the history of man if it wasn't her, given the fact that she's the honey bun of the drug lord at the hacienda, who just happens to have the strongest motive for wanting those papers of yours, which just happen to pinpoint the diamond mine, which just happens to be on his property."

Jack narrowed his gaze, as if he was mulling over what she'd said. She had the distinct feeling there was something he wasn't telling her, but he didn't elaborate and she had no way of knowing what to probe.

Finally, he said, "Kandy told me they weren't together any more. So why would she run around endangering herself on his behalf?"

Madison shrugged. "She lied. At the time she told you that, she was hot for your bod, and she lied so you'd still..." There was no delicate way to put it. "So you'd still play horizontal bingo with her."

He lifted a dark eyebrow. "Play what?"

"Never mind. The important thing is that she lied to you."

"No way," he scoffed. "And whether or not she lied, she's hardly the type to go around committing burglaries."

"Why not? Jack, let's not be blind here, okay? It all fits perfectly and you know it. You said the gunman had small feet, and might be a woman," she reminded him. "Plus you said it was a very stupid person. That's our Kandy."

"I hate it when you're right," he mumbled.

"And the jealousy thing makes sense, too." This part made her want to toss her cookies, but she continued anyway, trying to be persuasive for the greater good of their sleuthing endeavor. "Kandy was very enamored of you, and then some," she said tartly. "If she saw you and me together, in a position that made it seem like we might be becoming..." She cleared her throat "...more than friends, shall we say? Anyway, she might have decided a little gunfire was in order to break things up. I mean, I can't see her being thrilled to hang out on the balcony while we performed erotic gymnastics on the sofa."

Both eyebrows shot up.

"So she fired off a few rounds, gave us a good scare and made off with your papers," she said. *Erotic gymnastics*. Why had she said that, anyhow? Around Jack, anything was enough to incite riots in her nervous system.

But she didn't have time to be trembling and quivering. Jack seemed bent on some sort of mission. Brows together, he looked determined, resolute, passionately angry, as he grabbed her hand and dragged her back down the hall.

"I don't appreciate being towed like a house trailer," she complained, digging in her heels, trying to pull her hand away. But he kept on walking. When they reached the elevator, he dropped her hand, leaving her there, while he stomped back into her suite, emerging after only a few seconds with what looked like a small phone book.

"What's that?" she asked. "What are you doing?"

"It's the hotel directory. And I'm getting an elevator." He poked the button sharply.

"But why? She's long gone, Jack," Madison told him. "There's no point in trying to follow her now."

"She's not necessarily gone." Using his thumb, he pressed on the button again, this time for a long interval. "Remember, she had the cart."

"So? She could've dumped that anywhere in the hotel. She could've just left it on the elevator."

But the elevator doors slid open with a cheerful ping, revealing a square mirrored space, empty of laundry carts or anything else.

"Let's go," he ordered, pulling her onto the elevator with him.

"And where exactly are we going?"

"Where a maid would be likely to go." He thumbed through the pages of the hotel directory. "Management offices and housekeeping, third floor. I'm betting Kandy is somewhere near there."

She didn't know whether she hoped he was right or wrong. If Kandy had been the shooter, then Kandy still had a gun. And she could shoot at them all over again if she had half a mind to.

"Half a mind. That's exactly what she does have," Madison muttered, as the doors opened onto the quiet, dark and altogether spooky third floor of the hotel. Jack was already storming the citadel, and she was scared of the dark. "Jack, I don't think this is a good idea." She tapped his arm. "Jack? Do we really have to do this?"

"Come on, Mad, where's your spirit of adventure?" He took her hand in his, noiselessly guiding her down the empty hall, pausing only to peer at the titles on the doors. "I thought you were the one who liked getting shot at."

Trembling, Madison scooted in a little closer to Jack. "I didn't say I liked it. I never said I liked it. I said I didn't mind it, and then I even clarified that. So all I ended up saying was that I wasn't scared by it. But I'm definitely scared now. If only it weren't so empty here. Why aren't there any people?"

"Be quiet, will you? She's going to hear us coming."

"What's that?" Madison hissed, wheeling in the direction of a loud whoosh.

But it was only a soft-drink machine, wheezing to life in its own little niche built into the wall of the corridor. "A Coke machine," she murmured, trying to breathe again. "Just a silly machine."

She put her free hand over her chest to calm her heart, but it was still thumping out of control in there. Her breath was coming in short little gasps and she felt faint. All because of Kandy. She narrowed her eyes. She swore she was going to kill that bleached blond bimbo if she ever saw her again.

"I gave her my autograph," she grumbled. "I should've told her to take a flying leap."

Jack squeezed her hand gently. "This one," he said with satisfaction. He pulled to a stop in front of an office labeled Telemarketing, an office that looked like all the others on the floor. Except for the sliver of light glowing underneath the door. And there was a humming electric sound coming from inside, as if someone had fired up a clothes dryer or maybe an electric fan.

"Telemarketing?" Madison inquired. "Why here?"

Putting a finger to his lips to warn her to remain quiet, Jack eased the door open the barest of cracks. He stood there, looking inside, blocking her view for the longest time, until Madison began to feel very antsy. She could hardly use the usual methods of getting his attention, such as "What's going on?" in his ear or even the softest "pssst." So she tugged on his sleeve. And when he paid her no mind, she practically ripped his cuff off his shirt in an attempt to make her point.

Finally, he shut the door ever so carefully, one millimeter at a time, and then turned back to her. He stood there, tall and dark and intense, giving her the full brunt of his most forbidding gaze. "What is it now, Madison? Can't you stand here and behave yourself for three seconds?"

"What are you, the principal?" she whispered. "What the heck is going on in there, and why did you take so long?"

"I was trying to figure out what she was doing," he bit out.

"She? Then Kandy *is* in there?"

"A blond woman is in there. She's got her back to me and she's using some kind of machine, either a copy machine or a fax, I think."

"Do you think it's her?"

His jaw tightened. "It's her."

"Okay, so we found her. Now what?"

Jack shook his head, as if he was having trouble believing what he was hearing. "You're actually going to let me decide what we do next?"

"Well, no. Not if I don't like what you choose. But I'm sure you'll be sensible," she said helpfully.

"Oh, Mad. If I only knew what to do with you . . ."

"Do you want to burst in on her and make her confess?" she asked eagerly, tilting in closer to Jack.

He bent down, lowering his voice even further. "Not if she still has the ammo to blow us from here to kingdom come, which I think is a pretty good bet."

"Oh. Good thought. So do we wait for her to come out and then ambush her?"

Jack smiled, a small, sneaky one. "That's more what I was thinking. But let's hurry it up a little. Maybe some noise would do the trick. See if we can't get Kandy to come out and see what's up."

"What kind of noise?"

"Any kind." He rattled some change in his pocket as he retreated to the pop machine, and then extracted a few cans of Coke. Shaking them vigorously, he popped the tops, creating a loud explosion and a wide spray of sticky liquid, all over Madison.

"Yechh!" she cried, forgetting to keep her voice down. "You got Coke all over my shirt."

Jack tossed the still-full can casually at the telemarketing door. There was a bonk and a splash and lots of other good noises.

"What are you doing?" Madison demanded.

But he shoved her to one side of the door, the side it opened on, as he took up a station opposite her. It was just in time. The door slid open an inch or two and an eye appeared in the crack.

"Wha—" was all Madison had time to get out, as Jack reached for the door, ramming it open the rest of the way, knocking Kandy backward into the room as if she were a battering ram.

She sat there on the floor, still in the maid's uniform, with her mouth gaping open and her skirt twisted around her knees. It was not her most attractive position. The gun she'd apparently been carrying had skidded across the floor, stopping near Jack's foot. He picked it up and pointed it at Kandy without further ado.

"What the hell are you guys doin' here?" Kandy shrieked, signaling that she'd recovered her breath.

With a firm grasp on the gun, Jack hauled her to her feet and then slammed her into a nearby chair. "No tricks, Kandy. We know it was you upstairs. Now we want to know why."

"Huh? I ain't got no idea what you mean." She tried to rise from the chair, but Jack was right there to shove her back down.

"Spill it, Kandy," Madison said viciously. "Listen, sister, this is for real. Either you drop the dime and spill your guts, or we'll be all over you like a cheap suit."

"Madison," Jack interrupted in a quelling tone. "This is not a Cagney movie. Why don't I talk to Kandy while you scope out whatever it was she was doing over at the machine?"

"All right," she said primly. But she kept an ear peeled as she perused the stack of sheets Kandy had been sending off to who-knew-where. "It's a fax," she called out to Jack. "Plus she was using the shredder." Feeling forlorn, she let a mound of confetti slide through her fingers, displaying what was left of Jack's maps and diagrams. "Looks like she's already made her way through most of it before we got here. Sorry, Jack."

"I didn't do nothing," Kandy said sullenly.

"Nothing but destroy my papers and try to shoot us full of holes." He leaned toward the woman menacingly. "Why?"

"Nothing personal, babe." Kandy reached up to stroke Jack's cheek, but he moved away, leaving her and her scarlet nails hanging. "Just the cash. That's all I did it for."

"This is kind of out of your league, isn't it?"

"I've done stuff for Carlos before," she shot back. "Once I told him you was asking all those nosy questions about him and me and his place, it was like a favor to give me the gig."

"Were you supposed to kill us? Was that part of the bargain?" he asked, in a voice so cold and nasty Madison jumped way over on her side of the room.

"I didn't kill you, did I?" Kandy crossed her arms over her mammoth bosom, which was no mean feat, and looked at the floor. "It was just I seen you with that fancy writer lady, and I got kinda ticked off. You come on to me pretty good, and then you go doing it with her." She shook her bleached mane in disgust. "I was steamed."

"Yeah, well, I'm steamed, too," Jack growled. "Madison, do you have the rest of the papers collected together?"

"Yes," she said hastily. *Yes, sir!* She felt like she should salute as well, but she abandoned the idea. "What are you doing, Jack?"

As Madison watched, wide-eyed, he tucked the gun safely into his pocket and then ripped Kandy's uniform off her body. But his purpose became clear almost immediately, as Jack tore the fabric into several long strips, suitable for use as binding. Kandy was screaming bloody murder, wiggling and kicking, but Jack ignored her as he wrested her into place and lashed her down to the chair. After he was satisfied that the blonde and her heaving bosom were secure, he stepped back.

"Keep it down, will you? Somebody will find you in the morning. And we're going to leave a nice note to tell everybody what you did to the room upstairs, so you can pay for all that damage." Jack smiled down at Kandy. "Give Carlos our love, will you?"

And then he gagged her.

This was a bit beyond what Madison envisioned for her hero, even though she supposed Black Jack had done worse in his time, if she recalled properly. But that was fiction.

"Jack," she ventured, running to catch up. "Isn't that a little too...?" But she couldn't think of a good word.

"Too mean? Too ugly? Too horrible?" Jack's face was a study in fury. His dark eyebrows slashed down over blazing eyes, and his jaw was clenched so tightly Madison wondered how he could keep it that way without a good deal of pain. "Get used to the real world. This is it."

"But, Jack—"

"No buts," he said fiercely. "This has gone on too long. We get back what's mine and we do it now. No more time for games."

"Jack, I don't really think the papers that she shredded are that important. There are only a few we don't have copies of."

He was starting to scare her, with his thunderous face and his terrible disposition. His reaction seemed all out of proportion to the information Kandy had provided, and much too personal for the loss of a few papers. She was reminded of Bambi's father, looming there at the crest of a hill, antlers at the ready, raring to butt the tar out of some other stag. Jack's reaction seemed like that—like a macho turf war. But that made no sense at all. Did it?

Madison put a tentative hand on his arm. "What is this really about, Jack?"

"It's about getting out of Seattle, as fast as we can."

"We?"

His level gaze was a challenge, a dare. "I thought you were in for the long haul."

Madison swallowed around an obstruction in her throat. *He's inviting me to come with him.* "I'm in," she said clearly. "All the way."

"Fine. Get your stuff together. I'll arrange transportation." His eyes were so dark they looked more black than gray. "We're leaving tonight."

"YOU *BORROWED* A LEAR JET? And a pilot, too?" Madison's stomach plummeted. People could go to prison for kidnapping pilots and borrowing Lear jets. "Are you out of your mind?"

"Yeah. I'm taking a page out of your book."

"There are no jets in my books," she said wearily, trying to decide if fastening her seat belt meant she was an accessory after the fact. Fiddling with the crocheted edge of her white sweater, Madison frowned at Jack, who was ignoring the evil eye she was sending his way.

Seat belt or not, she was already on the damn plane, and that was bad enough. She'd never been inside a private jet before, and she had to admit it was very comfortable, all done in sea greens and blues, with plush swivel chairs opposite each other and a small couch across the back. But comfy or not, this was a joyride and patently illegal.

"My books take place between 1864 and 1874," she told him. "All of them. Unless I want Black Jack to stumble over a time machine, there are no jets in my books."

"Madison," he said in a chilly, unamused voice, "taking a page out of someone's book means acting like them. It doesn't mean removing pages from their actual, literal work."

"Well, of course." She blinked. "I knew that."

The plane lurched off the runway, and Madison quickly snapped her seat belt into place. So she was an accessory. She could always say that, like the pilot, she'd been kidnapped, forced to accompany this lunatic Black Jack.

"Well, you know, you did copy what I'd written before, with all that 'With me there's no middle ground' stuff, so I would've been perfectly justified in assuming that you'd literally lifted a page out of one of my books." She lifted her chin, trying to ignore the fact that the plane was roaring as it continued to climb skyward, that the bright lights of Seattle were spinning out there. "I guess my dialogue was so good you couldn't resist filching a little, hmm?"

"Don't flatter yourself, Mad." Jack spun his chair around to face out the window. "I used your dialogue because I knew it would work on you, not because I thought it was so all-fired great."

"Oh, sure. Right." She pursed her lips. It really annoyed her that he couldn't just give her the darned compliment and be done with it. No, he had to hold back, bite his tongue, just to deprive her of a kind word. "You're insufferable," she accused. "Admit it—you liked my books."

He shrugged, lifting those gorgeous shoulders only slightly. "They were okay."

"Okay? Okay?" Madison began to feel her internal heat rise. "I don't care what you say, Jack, or whatever your name is. My books are darned good—better than good—they're great! And you can just admit it."

But he wasn't looking at her, and he didn't seem to be in the least affected by her tirade. "Your books are okay, Madison," he said impatiently. He'd been in a cranky mood ever since he'd hustled her onto this stupid plane, and it didn't seem to be improving. "Drop it, will you?"

"They're better than that," she retorted, but her words were cut off by a stark flash of lightning outside Jack's window, illuminating the entire cabin of the plane for a full three seconds.

On the heels of the light show, a huge crackle and ferocious rumble sounded, as if the heavens themselves were breaking apart. And then another jagged bolt of lightning ripped the sky.

Madison flinched. "Are planes supposed to fly in this sort of weather?"

As if in answer, the planc took a dip, and so did Madison's stomach.

"It's just turbulence," Jack said easily, but Madison saw a look in his eyes she was sure belied his words. "Nothing to worry about."

"Nothing to worry about?" Madison screwed her eyes closed as lightning crackled on the other side of the small airplane, too. She felt so fragile, so unprotected, sailing along in this tiny plane, taking her chances in a sky filled with unbelievable hazards. "What if we're struck by lightning?"

"Planes are hit by lightning all the time. It doesn't do a damn thing. Here," he offered, sliding the shade down over his window, "we'll cover it up."

"I can still hear it," she insisted. "And I can still feel it. All this whooping and bucking. I feel like I'm on a roller coaster."

"That's hardly new," Jack said dryly. "You've been on a roller coaster since I met you."

She pulled herself together with difficulty. "It might surprise you to hear that I led a very normal life until I met you."

Blocking out the storm raging outside, Madison concentrated on Jack and his inane comments. There was plenty of turbulence inside, too, and she might as well deal with that first.

"I write books," she said plainly. "That's all I do. Before I got this stupid case of writer's block, I never had time to run around and get into trouble like you do. Thugs knocking you over the head and people shooting at you! You're the one with the roller coaster, not me."

"Yeah, well, maybe you needed a little roller coaster."

Madison slapped a hand onto her armrest. "What? What's that supposed to mean? You're the one who keeps telling me to go home and be safe."

"I'm just thinking of your books, Mad." His narrow lips curved into a mocking smile. "I'm sure it would put a real kick into your writing if you knew what you were talking about."

"Are you implying I don't?"

"Draw your own conclusions, Mad," he said evenly.

She tore off her seat belt, advancing on him unsteadily, weaving as the plane buffeted in the storm. "Why do you keep harping on my books?" she demanded. "What's wrong with my books?"

"Oh, that's right," he said acidly. He leaned back lazily, easing his chair back and forth. "I forgot that your books are sacred, taboo, off-limits. Wasn't that it?"

"You forgot sacrosanct," she snapped, lurching forward, almost tripping on his outstretched legs.

"But you know, Mad," he went on, in that same nasty, infuriating tone, "you really ought to learn to take criticism. I've read all your books now, you know, and I think you need to learn to do research."

"Research?" she returned. "Are you saying there's something wrong with my research?"

"What's wrong is that your books sound like you don't do any."

"Tell me this, Jack," she said, gritting her teeth. "Are you trying to be obnoxious, or is this your way of getting my mind off the damn storm?"

Thunder roared everywhere around them, as if to punctuate her words. But Madison was too angry to be cowed by the tempest outside. If she could've harnessed one of those lightning bolts for a little while, she would've zapped Jack where he sat, all lazy grace, all indolent charm. Leaning over him, she flipped the shade up with a sharp slap, letting the storm's sound and fury blast back into the cabin.

Jack caught her wrist in an iron grip, forcing her to turn and face him. "It's not my fault if your books are a bunch of hot air," he growled.

"Examples," she spat out, practically shouting over the thunderous din. "I want examples!"

"The love scenes." His eyes flashed to hers, and she saw the fire in their smoky depths.

Suddenly, the mood inside the cabin shifted, sweeping Madison into a quieter, more dangerous place, out of the path of the storm outside, but with another, bigger tempest just around the corner. The air around her had become heavy and humid, very still, full of sticky promise and hot intentions, as if she and Jack were standing in the eye of a hurricane, playing chicken, seeing who'd dash to safety first.

"The love scenes, Madison," he said again. His voice was a rough whisper, ruffling her nerve endings, top to bottom. "Don't you think you'd like a little sizzle in your love scenes, Mad?"

"Sizzle?" she managed, feeling very daring. "How about the steak?"

Excitement held her. Desire teased her. The idea of making love with Jack consumed her, down to the core of her being. She breathed deep, but she couldn't seem to get enough air.

She wanted him, and she wanted him now.

And then the lightning crashed and the thunder boomed, and the entire jet careered to one side. Madison fell headlong into Jack's lap and she held on, tangling her arms around his neck, pressing herself into him as closely as she could get.

She covered his mouth with hers, singeing him with a kiss full of longing and desperation and fear. With her hands clasped to his face, she whispered, "Put your money where your mouth is, Jack."

"I have better things to do with my mouth."

Chapter Eleven

The dark surrounded him like a shroud. Black Jack eased forward, kneeling to insert the pick into the padlock as quietly as he could manage. It wouldn't do to alert the palace guard that there was an intruder in their midst.

But then he had the lock, and then the next, until he was outside the door to the tower. Hesitating a moment, he listened intently. All he heard were the muted sounds of a woman's sobs.

He broke inside.

"Jack," she whispered, turning. "I didn't dare let myself dream . . ."

"Henriette, is that you?" he asked, squinting into the dark chamber where the Queen of Ruritania had been held a virtual prisoner for so many weeks.

"Yes, yes," she cried, throwing herself into his arms.

He crushed her to him. “Now all we have to do is get you out of here.”

Black Jack Brogan, Book #15
Jack the Whip

“Do you know what I want to do with my mouth, Madison?” he asked, nipping at her lips, tracing the slender line of her throat and her collarbone as her head tipped back.

Her beautiful green eyes were alive with spirit and desire, flashing fire as vibrant as the lightning reflected there. He felt her tremble in his arms, and her lips parted slightly as she tried to breathe more deeply, her breasts rising and falling with the effort. Still she held on to him, moving around to straddle his lap more closely, making his body throb with desire underneath her.

“Madison,” he murmured, framing her face with his hands, brushing his lips ever so lightly across her cheeks and her eyelids and her chin. “You're playing with fire.”

“All my life,” she said huskily, kissing him hungrily, soft and then hard and then soft again, just a whisper of her sweet lips. She smiled as she brushed the tip of her finger very lightly against the tiny cleft in his chin. “All my life I've wanted to feel what it would be like to make love with you.”

Shifting in his lap, her thighs barely grazed him, but the movement fanned the fires inside him even higher.

"Please, Jack. Right here, right now," she said breathlessly.

His body had gone rigid under her. Did she know what she did to him?

"Slow down." He took a deep breath. "We have to slow down."

"I don't want to slow down," she told him. Her small hands traveled restlessly over his collar and his sleeves, as if she was willing his clothes to disappear. And then she cupped his face with her hands, brushing against the shadow of his beard, kissing him long and deep, with sweetness and joy and innocence. It made him crazy.

It gave him pause. "I can't do this," he said, pushing her hands away, pushing her away.

As she sat there at the edge of his lap, her eyes were wide with distress. She ruffled her hair through her fingers in the nervous gesture she used sometimes. "Jack," she said hoarsely, sliding her palms over his shoulders, down the front of his shirt. "You made a promise to me." She paused, but her voice was still thready, uneven. "When we were getting shot at and you were leaving, you told me you'd come back and make love to me." Her tongue flicked over her bottom lip. "For a long, long time."

He didn't need the reminder. Head to toe he ached to hold her, to touch her, to bury himself inside her until there was nothing in the world but Madison. He swore, tearing his eyes away from hers, staring instead at her Tweedledee and Tweedledum earrings.

Only Madison would be wearing Tweedledee and Tweedledum while she was in the middle of a seduction scene. He fingered one of them, wishing he had the capacity to laugh at his own folly. But it hurt too much to laugh, looking at those silly little earrings, knowing what sort of person he was involved with, realizing yet again how much she amused him and how much, deep down, he really liked Madison.

She was goofy and she was a nuisance, but she was completely and irrevocably herself. And she had more moxie and more irrepressible charm in her little finger than any ten people of his acquaintance.

He realized suddenly that from the first moment he'd met her, he had been enchanted by her free spirit. Madison had the courage of her convictions and enough energy and enthusiasm to charge straight ahead, no matter what. For the first time in his life, he felt real affection for a woman. He really cared what she thought of him and how she would feel when he walked away.

And now his newfound integrity was going to be put to the test, and he was going to have to be more noble than he'd ever been. He was going to have to let her go.

"I made that promise when I thought we were both going to die," he explained carefully. But they were no longer teetering on the brink of death. Now she was safe and it was up to him to keep her that way. He had to protect her, to keep her damn illusions intact. Didn't he?

He swore under his breath, turning away enough to gaze out the window at a bright flash of lightning. There were times when Madison's smile seemed to light up as the sky, as bright and as lively as this amazing electrical storm.

And then there were the other times, when she seemed youthful and naive, as if she'd been sheltered her entire life. How else to explain the way she'd followed him and let herself get caught in the alley? Or the way she'd barged into what she called his "caper," as if life and death were merely fun and games? Any woman who'd been around would've known better than to leap into actions that were so dangerous, so foolish. But Madison continued undaunted, to take what she wanted and damn the consequences.

Was she that naive? Or just that fearless?

Or maybe, just maybe, she was the woman he'd glimpsed behind her books, the one who liked life fast and fiery. He closed his eyes, trying hard not to remember that she was there on his lap, while visions from her books filled his head, visions of Madison naked in a haystack, Madison upside-down in a laundry cart, Madison moist and hot around him in a stifling stagecoach that jolted her up and down, in a rhythm that was out of this world.

He broke out in a sweat.

No, it couldn't be. There was no future for them, and he knew Madison was not the sort of woman he could make love to and then leave behind. He also knew, even if she didn't, that he was still lying through his teeth about the reasons for all the maps and the diagrams. Worse than that, she didn't even know his name. It didn't seem to bother her, but it sure bothered him.

How could he make love to her under those circumstances? And yet, with his need for her growing more desperate with every second, how could he *not* make love to her?

"Madison," he ventured, floundering for some sort of answer. "How innocent are you?"

"How innocent do you want me?"

That took him aback. "No games, Madison," he said finally. "I just need to know."

A long pause hung between them. "You've read my books. What do you think?"

"I think you have a vivid imagination."

Her cheeks flamed, but he had no clue if the cause was anger or heightened desire. "Does this feel like your imagination, Jack?" she asked softly, leaning forward to lick the curve of his ear, to slide her hands inside his shirt, ripping it open, scattering his buttons like dust in the wind.

His heart hammered against his ribs.

"Does this look like your imagination, Jack?" she whispered, stripping off her sweater and tossing it backward over her head, revealing the sheerest of silk camisoles, slick to her skin, in a pale aqua that set off her ivory skin and brought out the green in her mischievous eyes.

His body stiffened with desire.

And then she reached for the lace hem of the camisole, inching it up, tantalizingly slow, until he saw the bottom curve of her bare breast.

Groaning low in his throat, he put out a hand to stop her, but all he touched was skin, glowing, sweet skin, as smooth as the silk of her discarded camisole. Her soft, round breast filled his hand, its rosy nipple peaking against his palm, and he knew he was undone.

Holding her fast, he swept them both off the chair and onto the carpeted floor of the small plane, rolling under her to shield her. But Madison was so absorbed in driving him out of his mind that she didn't let up, didn't even seem to notice that their positions had changed. Crouched over him, she bent to kiss him, sliding those soft, moist lips down and around the hard muscles of his chest, until he thought he might die.

Swiftly, he flipped her over, trapping her hips between his knees. And then, when she lay underneath him, one arm hooked around his neck to pull him back down to her, gazing up at him with dark, passion-dazed eyes, he smiled.

Forget about being noble. He was going for it.

He sat back far enough to shrug out of his shirt, throwing it away carelessly, and then he reached for the snap on her jeans. Pop. The sound was enough to make her gasp and to make his smile widen. He loved Madison when she was being wicked, but he loved her just as well when she lost a little of that self-possession.

"What are you grinning about?" she whispered.

"You." He tugged her jeans down and discarded them, enjoying for a long moment the sight of Madison wearing only a skimpy pair of aqua panties. "You're adorable."

"I'd rather be sexy or beautiful or exotic," she said wistfully. "I'm not complaining, Jack, but just once I'd love to be beautiful."

"Madison," he chided softly. "Don't you know? You're always beautiful." He drew one finger down her bare thigh, watching her quiver in response. "You're gorgeous. You're so completely yourself, Madison." His finger skimmed higher, sliding under the thin ribbon at the side of her panties. "I can't believe how beautiful that makes you."

She closed her eyes and took a deep breath. "Did I write that?" she gasped.

"No," he said firmly. "I made it up myself."

"Oh," she breathed. "Good."

Quickly he pulled Madison up, cradling her in the circle of his arms, holding her fast, as he'd wanted to for so long. With her bare skin pressed next to his, he could feel her heart beating as erratically, as crazily as his own. He pressed a swift kiss into the curve of her neck. "You continue to amaze me."

"Don't stop now," she said, shivering.

"I'm not planning to."

With his arms hard around her, he found her mouth, nipping her tongue and her teeth and then plunging inside, hot, harsh, demanding, knowing Madison would give back as good as he gave. He couldn't get enough. The kiss went on and on, until they were both dizzy with need and oxygen deprivation.

When she broke away, stroking his back with her slender hands, kneading him and exciting him, he bent his head, teasing her passion-darkened nipples with his mouth, first one and then the other, until she moaned his name and slid back all the way to the floor. He followed, covering her body with his, tangling their legs together, spinning over and over like the rolling thunder outside.

Madison nipped at his lips, stopping their motion so that she lay completely underneath him. Her hands framed his head, stroking his hair, as she whispered something incoherent and delicious. He couldn't resist bending to taste her and caress her, all of her, but he wondered how long he could last this way, aching for her touch on the hardest, neediest part of him, dying to take the final step, to fit his body to hers completely.

"Jack," she murmured, her hands at the top button of his jeans, fumbling to unfasten them. "Jack, please..."

He pulled back to breathe, take air in deeply. He wanted to take his time, to make it good for her. After all, she'd been living with the ghost of Black Jack all these years, and he was going to have to go some to compare to that paragon of perfection. But he couldn't keep himself in control. He felt like a kid again, panting after a cheerleader under the bleachers.

He tried to rein himself in, to pace himself, but she wasn't having any of it. Her fingers edged one button and then two through the denim slits, pressing the issue.

"I want to touch you," she whispered, already moving on to the next button, pushing savagely at the cloth, driving him even farther down the road to madness.

He batted her hand away, but it fluttered right back, until she had all the buttons undone, and she cupped him through the black fabric of his briefs, tracing his length. He couldn't hold back. It had gone too far, too fast, and he had to have her. Now.

But he gave her one last chance to do the right thing.

"Madison," he said roughly, "are you sure?"

"Jack," she snapped back, "I'm sure. Absolutely, positively sure. If you make me wait one more second, I'm going to kill you. Okay?"

He nodded.

"Good." And she slid her hand inside his jeans.

Caught up in that one fierce moment, he shoved his clothes away, kicking them off. Without pausing, he divested Madison of the remnants of her clothing, those sinful little panties.

And then it was just the two of them, with nothing in between. She was slippery and hot, and he was so ready it hurt.

"Come to me, Jack," she said. And he held her close for a moment and then slipped inside.

She was more wonderful than anything he'd ever felt in his life, rising to meet him, murmuring soft words, wrapping her legs around him and urging him in deeper and deeper. Under him, she writhed and sighed and made soft moans. He stroked and she tightened around him, and he knew he couldn't last long.

"Madison," he tried. But it was too late.

His passion crested, and he fell headlong into a climax of shattering power. Earth-shattering. Heartbreaking.

Madison shouted "Jack" so loudly that it shocked him, collapsing against him, and he could see the waves of pleasure reverberate in her wide green eyes. With her reaction and his combined it was like being at the center of an earthquake, and he felt weak in the aftershock.

"Amazing..." she purred, still moving against him, and he dropped his forehead to hers, tangling his fingers in the short, silky tendrils at the back of her neck. Her hair was wet and slick with perspiration, and her pale skin shone pink where his beard had rasped against her. Telltale evidence of the bonfire they'd built together.

He was unwilling to accept the magnitude of what had just happened. This wasn't just sex, even though it was the best he'd ever had. He'd had it last longer, and he'd done it in more exotic places, but far and away this was the best.

But what had happened between him and Madison wasn't even about sex. No, this was a cataclysm, a revelation. A shock.

I love her, he thought, damning himself for ever letting things get this far. *I've never had sex like this before, I've never felt anything like this before, and I love her.*

God help me, I love Madison Talley. But now what did he do?

He held her closer, unable to let go, unable to tell her what he'd discovered. Trust Madison to be way ahead of him.

"I love you, Jack," she said gently. She bit her lip, gazing up at him with such trust, such obvious love, that he knew he was in big trouble. "Don't worry, you don't have to say anything back."

"My name's not Jack," he began, but she cut him off, giving him one last kiss.

And then the landing gear creaked and groaned under them, reminding them for the first time in a long time that there was an outside world to be contended with.

"Coming down," the pilot's voice announced from the cockpit. "Two-minute warning, folks."

He was almost glad for the interruption, feeling very uneasy about whatever it was that had happened here. But Madison appeared less pleased. She blushed a becoming shade of rose pink, as Jack hurried to toss over her white sweater and jeans.

"How much do you think the pilot heard?" Madison inquired, her flush deepening.

Jack struggled into his own jeans, no easy feat when the plane was bouncing and skipping to a rough landing. "There's a door in between, so we should've been okay," he said in a hard, cynical tone he hadn't intended. "But neither of us was making any effort to be quiet."

The color in her face had graduated to a scarlet shade. "I've never done anything like this before in my life," she said weakly, tucking in her camisole and yanking her sweater over her head.

"Yeah, but you've got a vivid imagination." Smiling in spite of himself, Jack shook his head at the puzzle that was Madison. She'd attacked him like a tigress, and now she was embarrassed.

"It must have been the storm," she muttered. "I'm sure that's it. The storm just got to me. You know, all that natural electricity and barometric pressure and stuff. But everything seems to have calmed down now. Weatherwise, I mean." She raked both hands through her hair, rearranging her spiky do, and then sent him a surreptitious glance. "Did you notice the storm was over?"

"I noticed."

"We're here," the pilot shouted.

There was no time for further conversation as they busied themselves gathering up their bags and getting ready to get off the "borrowed" plane. Jack hid another smile. Madison had been in such a dither, thinking he'd stolen it, that he hadn't had the heart to tell her it was his plane.

Good ol' Madison. Life was certainly entertaining with her in it.

THE PARADISE MOTEL was worse than Madison had remembered. "Why do we have to stay here?" she asked for the seventeenth time. She peered around the curtain into the dusty, grimy street. "My hotel was a lot nicer, and I can afford the difference in the cost even if you can't."

"Everybody here has something to hide. That makes it safer for us to hide out, too," he said tersely.

"I don't like it here," she persisted, casting a hungry eye at the way Jack's strong muscles bunched and unbunched under the black T-shirt he was wearing. The bed was so close and Jack was so very near.... She sighed. Her hands trembled with the need to touch him and she jammed them into the pockets of her shorts, not trusting herself. "Jack, did you hear me?"

But she knew he wasn't really paying attention—he was too intent on making new squiggly lines next to the old squiggly lines on his map, too intent on pretending their little diversion on the jet had never happened.

"Madison, are you sure you can handle this?" he asked for the twenty-fifth time. He glanced up from his work.

"Yes," she told him impatiently, edging away from his gaze. "Do you want to hear the drill? We go after dark, we wear our nifty black outfits, we sneak into Mexico and then we carefully bypass all the alarm systems and the dogs at the hacienda, all of which we hope are clearly noted on Map *A*, or we are in deep doodoo."

He did not appear amused, but she continued anyway. "Then you crack the safe with your handy burglar tools while I stand watch. And after we have your files, we make our way by hook or by crook to Laredo, where we come back across the border with eight million other people, so no one will notice." She shrugged. "Nothing to it. I've seen *To Catch a Thief* a million times. We play Cary Grant, we get in, we get out. It's a snap."

"This isn't a movie, Madison, and neither of us is Cary Grant."

"I can do it, Jack."

"I ought to have my head examined," he muttered.

So should I, Madison thought morosely. This wasn't turning out at all as she'd planned. Oh, she was getting a dandy caper, all right. She couldn't have expected anything nearly as exciting as playing cat burglar at a mysterious hacienda. But Jack... She sighed heavily, and he looked up at the sound.

Smiling weakly, she thought about them rolling around on the floor of that plane without any clothes on, and her stomach did the minute waltz. She had to sit down or faint. When she thought about the feel of Jack's hands, the warmth of his mouth, her whole body began to throb and pulsate. She feathered her bangs with her fingers, blowing air onto her face, but it didn't help. She was already overheated and he hadn't even touched her in twenty-four hours.

A quick look at her watch updated that estimate. "Twenty-five hours and three minutes," she said disconsolately.

"What?"

"Nothing."

She began to pace back and forth in front of the window. Had she really done that, really thrown herself at him ten thousand feet in the air? It was so unlike her, so shameful, so embarrassing, so needy....

Yet it had turned out to be absolutely perfect.

As she gazed at him, sitting there, poring over his damn diagrams, she knew she wasn't sorry. Making love with Jack had been the stuff of dreams—wonderful, terrific, unbelievable. Imagination, and all of her fictional love scenes put together, paled next to the real thing.

Now if only she knew what conclusions to draw. Did he care at all? Had it knocked him for a loop like it had her? Or was it just another notch in the bedpost for Black Jack Brogan?

"No," she said fervently. "It meant something. I know it did."

"What?"

"Nothing," she returned.

But when she replayed the torrid light in his eyes when she'd stripped off her sweater, she knew it had meant more than nothing to him. That night, she could honestly say he was as hot as she was. Madison smiled to herself. He'd wanted her as much as she'd wanted him.

And still did. This thing was far from over.

She came up behind him, trying to decide if she should interrupt him. Hesitating, she chewed her lip.

"Madison," he said softly, "don't."

"Don't what?"

"Don't..." He swallowed with effort. "Don't anything. We have business to attend to. We agreed, hands off till after we get into Carlos's house, after we get back what's mine."

"And then?" she asked him. "After we get the files, what then?"

"I don't know."

It wasn't the answer she'd hoped for, no declaration of undying love, not even a declaration of undying lust, but it would do for the moment.

"Maybe I don't know either, Jack," she said with an edge of impatience. "Maybe, when all is said and done, this won't be your decision."

His eyes were a soft, somber gray as he gazed at her. "Maybe it won't."

"I guess we'll just have to see."

"I guess we will," he murmured.

She glanced down at her watch. "Almost time to put on the black clothes, Jack."

"Almost time."

Madison reached for her black turtleneck. Just like in the movies. And maybe when they were done, when they had retrieved whatever it was that was so all-fired important to Jack, she'd have her answer.

Or maybe at least he'd touch her again.

Madison closed her eyes, pressing Jack's shirt to her nostrils. It still smelled like him.

He has to touch me again, she told herself. *I'll kill him if he doesn't.*

SHE COULD HEAR THE DOGS barking already, a series of deep, mournful howls that echoed in the hot, still night. And they weren't even over the wall.

"Why are they barking? Do they smell us?" she whispered.

"Maybe they just like to bark."

She scratched at the collar of her black turtleneck, swamped with heat and humidity. The trickle of sweat between her breasts was turning into a river, and wearing so many clothes was like torture. She itched everywhere.

"Stop fidgeting," Jack ordered.

He was ahead of her, fastening some sort of hook to get them over the high security wall, so how in heck did he know *what* she was doing?

"Come on," he said sharply. "Up and over."

She hadn't climbed like this since junior high gym class, but she found muscles she didn't know she had, inching up until she successfully straddled the top of the fence. Jack was right behind her, but he didn't stop, just vaulted over onto the hard, dry ground inside Carlos's citadel.

The dogs continued to bellow, louder and scarier, and Madison began to get a bad feeling about those hounds. She had visions of being torn limb from limb by pit bulls. "Where are they?" she asked, sticking to her perch, peering into the darkness. "I thought their pen was way over on the other side."

"Maybe they're loose."

She shot an alarmed glance down at him. "You're kidding, right?"

"Madison, they're behind a fence, okay? Look." He switched on his flashlight, quickly sweeping a tall chain-link fence with the beam. Huge doggie faces with slobbering tongues and red eyes pressed against the fence from the other side. "See the fence?"

"Yes, I see the fence, but those dogs are hideous."

"You're safe, okay? Get down here."

Taking a deep breath, she decided she had no choice. She couldn't very well sit on the fence all night. After a small mental pep talk, she jumped down, almost landing on her bottom, but recovering to scramble along behind Jack as he led the way to the house.

Slipping through the ominous darkness, they reached the terrace, a pretty tiled area with festive colored lanterns swaying in the negligible breeze. A tinkle of brass sounded softly, making Madison whip around in that direction.

"Oh," she said, relieved, "wind chimes."

"Come on." After snipping a tiny wire that ran around the doorframe, Jack picked a small lock, sliding open one side of the French doors. "So far, so good. That should take care of the first set of alarms."

Her heart was beating a rapid tattoo as Madison slipped in ahead of him, feeling her way with one hand. According to Jack's maps, they should be in the library, and indeed they were. High shelves of books, a few leather wing chairs and a maroon Persian rug were briefly illuminated as Jack shone his light around the handsome room.

"Not what I expected." She took a calmer breath, trying to feel safe now that they'd found their target. Fingering the books on a nearby shelf, she could make out Dickens and Thackeray, and the complete works of Shakespeare. "Good taste for a drug dealer," she said skeptically.

Meanwhile, Jack snipped a few more wires and then moved aside a dark painting of some aged person in doublet and ruff, revealing a safe right where it was supposed to be. "Bingo," he whispered.

And then he went to work. After attaching a small square box that looked like a digital clock, he fiddled with it for only a few moments until there was an audible click.

"That was quick."

"The wonders of modern science," he said with a brief smile. He swung open the thick metal door and began to pull out a stack of wide leather notebooks. "Here," he said, handing them over.

"But, Jack," Madison began, looking down at what he'd lumped into her outstretched arms. "These don't look anything like the ones I took, the ones you lost. They're huge."

But her words were cut short by a piercing wail from one side and a shrill siren from the other. "Holy smokes! What's that?"

"Alarms. We're busted," Jack said grimly.

Chapter Twelve

Faith had conked him over the head with a stew pot, and then she'd tied him to one of her kitchen chairs.

"But why?" he asked, struggling against her knots. "I care for you, Faith, and I thought you cared for me."

"I know who you are now," she said quietly. She pulled a crumpled paper out of her apron pocket, unfolding it to show him a Wanted poster. With his face on it. "Black Jack Brogan," she whispered. She raised haunted eyes to his. "I've sinned with Black Jack Brogan. What's to become of me now?"

He held himself very still. "You say that like you think I'm the devil himself," he growled.

Faith's round brown eyes held pity and contempt. "And isn't that exactly what you are?"

Black Jack Brogan, Book # 13
Every Man Jack

"But I thought you knew where the alarms were. I thought you took care of them."

Jack's jaw clenched. "I was afraid this was a little too easy. The only alarms I could get anybody to admit to were definitely minor-league stuff. I'm guessing our friend Carlos installed a more sophisticated system after the one I found out about." He shook his head. "Or maybe he fed me bad information on purpose."

Her heart began to pound. "Like he knew we were coming?"

"Exactly."

"What do we do?" Madison demanded, really starting to panic now. She moved a little closer to Jack, as if that would help.

"We get out of here," he said curtly.

He made a move for the French doors they'd used to come in, but skidded to a stop. The sounds of barking and roaring increased tenfold, as if the hounds of hell had suddenly gotten a lot closer. And as they watched, horrified, big dogs came crashing into the door from outside, hurling against it, yelping and howling.

"Those dogs know where we are," Madison said with a gulp. "They know, and they want to come in here and tear us to pieces." All she could think about was those awful, terrifying dog faces, slobbering to get at her. She tried not to whimper.

From upstairs, they could hear the noise of the big house coming to life—footsteps, voices, the clatter of questions and answers. Everywhere, there was noise. Everywhere, there was danger.

"Come on," Jack said harshly, grabbing her hand and heading out of the library.

But Madison halted two steps into the hallway. "But what if this is the way they're coming? We'll run right into them."

They hesitated there, looking left and then right, neither sure of which way to go.

"We'll have to split up." He took all but one of the heavy notebooks, and then started to offer rapid instructions. "I'll go toward the front and you go the other way, through the kitchen and up the servants' stairs. Wait until things quiet down a little, then double back and go out the front door. Do you remember the maps of the house and the grounds?"

She nodded, trying to picture it in her mind. Everything was a blur, a panicked, hazy blur. But she had no intention of telling Jack that.

"Good," he said. "I'll meet you in the garden. There should be a gardener's shack at the back, not far from the fountain. Find the fountain, then go to the shack. I'll be there. Okay?"

"Okay." She was scared to death. But she had to play her part. Only by gritting her teeth and running like hell was she going to get out of this alive. "Okay," she repeated, in a quaking voice. "I can do it."

"Good girl, Mad. That's it, then."

She nodded again. Wrapped up in her instructions, clutching her notebook, she moved to go, but he pulled her back and kissed her fiercely, briefly. Too briefly.

As he pushed away, he whispered, "I love you."

She looked up, shocked, but he was already gone, slipping soundlessly around a corner and out of sight. The alarms were blaring with renewed force, the dogs sounded like they were going to rip the doors down with their teeth, people were shouting in Spanish, and she had no choice. She had to run.

But as she scrambled up the stairs, ducking down a servants' hall, there was only one thought on Madison's mind.

He loves me.

MADISON WAS LOST. Good and lost. The inside of this hacienda was like a maze, and she had no idea where she'd been or how to get back to the stairs.

She swiped the bangs back from her brow, wishing she knew what to do next. *Upstairs,* he'd said, and then something about coming back down the stairs on the other side so she could escape out the front door while everyone was running after Jack.

Jack. Oh, dear. Jack. Her heart lodged in her throat, as she prayed to any deity listening. *Let him be okay. You can't let him die after he just told me he loves me.*

"He loves me," she said softly, savoring the words on her lips. With that kind of incentive, she could find her way out of Hacienda Carlos blindfolded, couldn't she?

Unless he'd been lying. In her heart, she wanted to believe him, but her head kept playing tricks on her, telling her she was being foolish, that a man like Jack was about as likely to fall for her as fly to the moon.

But if that was true, why would he have bothered to tell her he loved her?

"Maybe he was just being nice. Maybe he thinks we're both going to die and he wants me to go to my maker happy, like I'm better off thinking something schmaltzy as I go to that big roundup in the sky." Her brain added, *As if once you're dead, it matters,* just to be snide.

"No, that's not it," she told herself severely. "He's not even remotely a nice person, and he wouldn't say something like that out of pity. I know him better than that." She held on tightly to the notebook. "I hope I know him better than that."

But then she went stock-still. She had distinctly heard noises from inside a room she'd just passed, noises that indicated people were coming out any minute. Her blood pressure went into overdrive as she stood there in the middle of the hall, trying to decide where to hide.

Swiftly, she sneaked into an open doorway far enough to stay out of sight. Just in time. Three guards carrying rifles tromped right past her without noticing a thing.

"Oh, brother," she moaned. That had been a little too close for comfort. She took a couple of steady breaths before tiptoeing out far enough to make sure they were gone.

Safe for the moment, anyway.

But where was Jack? Moreover, where was she? She'd glanced briefly at all the maps and diagrams in his rooms, trying to prepare herself for cat burglary, but these hallways and staircases didn't correspond to anything she remembered. And when she'd been traipsing around, trying desperately to stay out of sight, she hadn't paid attention to what floor she was on, or what path she'd used to get there.

It was difficult to be sensible about leaving a trail or memorizing her surroundings when everywhere she turned there were clusters of armed guards. Unless she was one step ahead of the same set of guys again and again, this place was better fortified than San Quentin. Several times she'd just headed a different direction when she heard them on her heels again. At least someone had thought to turn off the damn alarms at some point and she could hear herself think again.

But by now she was so twisted up and turned around she had no idea which direction the front of the house was, let alone how to get there. She had visions of Jack seething out there in the gardener's shack, cooling his heels while she ran around in circles in here. Or would he be horribly worried, imagining that she'd fallen into the hands of the bad guys, when all she really was was confused?

"Damn it," she muttered. "I wish I had a better sense of direction."

If this were one of her books, the heroine would have an unerring instinct, a sort of internal radar, to lead her right back to Black Jack. Unfortunately, Madison had no internal or external radar. Nothing.

And inside the hacienda there was no convenient moss on a tree, or even a bright star, to point her in the right direction. She'd now been through the kitchen twice, in four or five bathrooms, past so many empty bedrooms she'd lost count, and—she closed her eyes with terror even now, as she remembered—she'd even wandered through a room where a chubby woman was sleeping in a chair.

God only knew who the woman was or how she'd managed to doze on peacefully through all the brouhaha currently taking place in the hacienda, but Madison wasn't about to question such a fortunate case of sleep. She'd ducked out of that room on the double, skating into another sitting room and from there back out into the hall.

But what hall? What floor?

"Where am I?" she asked in frustration. She took a quick peek into the room whose doorway she'd used as a hiding place, but it was as dark and empty as all the rest.

Backtracking, she decided she'd check out the place the guards had come from. Maybe one of them had left a map, or better yet, a weapon, at their station. Even a window would be helpful, so she could look outside and get her bearings. The only problem would be if there were more guards where the first three had come from.

She found the door they'd come out of easily enough, but it opened onto a small antechamber with yet another door. And the second door was closed, with light and sounds coming out from under it. If she pressed her ear up against it, she could hear the funny noises more clearly. They sounded like pings and boings bouncing at rhythmic intervals, or maybe some kind of carnival music. What the heck was that?

She simply couldn't think of any explanation for that bizarre collection of sounds. Gathering her courage, Madison pushed the door open an inch or two, as silently as she could manage in case there was someone inside.

There was. He was wearing a guard's cap like all the others, but he was facing away toward a whole wall full of TV monitors and he was puffing on a cigar, blowing nasty clouds of smoke over his head.

Amazed, Madison just stared, taking it all in. Clearly, this was the surveillance room, with the monitors recording everything that happened in the mansion. She couldn't see much detail from where she stood, but there appeared to be at least thirty monitors, some of them reflecting grainy black and white and some of them bright video floor plans with blinking red and blue lights.

The one smack dab in front of the guard was a video monitor, but that was no floor plan he was looking at. It was glowing with brightly colored cartoon characters, including a gorilla who was jumping up and down and beating his chest.

It's a video game, she realized. The guard was sitting there, in the middle of a break-in, smoking a foul cigar and playing Donkey Kong! Every time he scored a point or found a banana or something, the screen flashed and made those same funny noises she'd heard from outside. In fact, there was a whole soundtrack of perky little video-game noises, explaining what she'd thought was carnival music.

This guy wouldn't have heard her coming if she'd brought the entire Marine Corps band with her. Frowning with the effort, Madison raised her heavy notebook high over her head as she advanced on the guard. At the last possible moment, she screwed up her courage and bonked him hard.

"Ooof," he said, or something similar, as he slumped to the side. His cigar fell out of his mouth and landed on the linoleum, while his monitor made sorrowful noises. The cartoon ape jumped up and down, telling him to start a new game.

"Game over," Madison announced cheerfully. Quickly, she pushed him off his chair and neatly squashed his cigar in the overflowing ashtray next to his computer games. Stepping over him, she gingerly removed his gun from his holster and then bonked him again, to make sure he'd stay out for a while. But that still didn't seem entirely safe. She spotted a utility closet handy and after much effort managed to shove and drag him into the closet, which she promptly locked from outside. She also locked the door into the surveillance room, so nobody could run in and surprise her.

And then she plunked herself down in his chair and began to search the monitors for signs of Jack. The monitors didn't get very clear pictures, but she did catch glimpses of guards patrolling here and there. But not Jack. Not in the hallways, not in the bedrooms, not in the kitchen. No Jack.

Everything in the surveillance room was labeled, which was very helpful of them, Madison thought. She noted buttons marked Alarms, that could be flicked on and off; a set called Locks, with different rooms labeled, which apparently meant you could lock and unlock most of the rooms in the hacienda from the master console; plus a very nice intercom system with all the various speaker locations neatly noted.

She fiddled with a variety of switches, figuring out how to turn things on and off, how to adjust the sound and the picture on the monitors and how to switch them from surveillance to video, in case she wanted to play games like the guard in the closet. But each monitor showed only one location, with no ability to change the location showing. And unfortunately, Jack wasn't in any of the rooms that showed up on the TVs. Finally, she'd tried every monitor in the room except the one where the guard's video game was still gently beeping.

"I wonder," she mused. "I changed the other ones from monitor to video. How about vice versa?"

Quickly, she flipped the switch on the Donkey Kong game, watching intently as it warmed up and slowly tuned itself in. Finally, after what seemed like forever, it presented her with a fuzzy picture of the library.

"Oh, Jack," she whispered.

There he was, tied to a chair in the library, while a heavyset man with a leonine mane of hair pointed a gun at him. She could see Jack fairly clearly, but only the back of the other man. She turned up the sound all the way, desperate to hear Jack's voice, to know that he was all right.

"Tell me," the other man commanded in a low, rough voice that was muffled because he wasn't pointed in the right direction. Still, if she concentrated, she could make out most of the words. "I want to know where the other nuff-nuff is."

Nuff-nuff? What the heck was that?

"That's all there was in the safe, Carlos," Jack mumbled. "You've got all I found."

Since all Jack had found were notebooks, Madison made a mental note to translate "notebook" for "nuff-nuff" from now on, whenever the man named Carlos spoke.

So this was Carlos, she mused, the mad drug lord who owned the hacienda. He didn't seem pleased to find himself with visitors. As Madison watched, the wretched man reached out and slugged Jack hard, whipping his head to one side.

Madison felt its impact punch her, too. She cried out, "No!" but there was nothing she could do.

"The notebook," Carlos repeated, breathing heavily. Wiping his mouth with his gun hand, he shifted to the side, and Madison shot forward in her seat.

"Marley?" she exclaimed. "It can't be!"

But it was. Carlos was really Marley, her old nemesis Marley, the same man who'd labored alongside her back in the old days, when they'd both been under contract to act as the voice of Roderick Tweed. But how could Marley be the person holding Jack prisoner and acting crazy about notebooks? Madison whirled, trying desperately to understand.

The last time she'd seen him, he was dressed as Marley's Ghost from "A Christmas Carol." Not this time. Now, he looked for all the world like a prosperous businessman in his pajamas. Except for the gun he was wielding so carelessly.

"What the hell is going on?" she asked the television.

She felt a rising need to dash back down to the library to try to save Jack. But how? She had the gun, and that might help, but at the moment she had no path to get back there. Even if she raced, even if she found a direct route to the library, by the time she got there Marley could've done his worst. And if she bolted out into the hall without thinking first, she'd probably run headfirst into a posse of guards, and then they'd both end up captured and smacked around by deranged Marley.

"I'd come if I could, Jack," she whispered, crashing back into her seat. Right now all she could do was watch and wait, bite her fingernails, stew and fret, turn over and over her options in her fevered brain.

"Who are you?" Marley demanded. "I know I've seen you before. Who are you?"

"You saw him at the costume ball, you dodo!" Madison shouted, up in her control room where no one could hear.

When Jack didn't answer, Marley tried, "Who's your partner, the woman? Where did she get off to?"

"I don't have a partner."

Slap. The back of Marley's hand cracked Jack's jaw. "My guards saw her," he grunted. "We know she's in the house somewhere. It's only a matter of time before we find her."

"That's what you think," Madison taunted him. "Your guards are too busy playing Donkey Kong. They couldn't find an elephant at the circus."

But somebody had found Jack, hadn't they? "I didn't bring anyone with me," he insisted, struggling against his bonds.

Marley shook his head, making his heavy hair stand on end, casting it out like a nimbus around him. "Why do you want my notebooks?" he asked suddenly. "What good are they to you?"

"I didn't want the damn notebooks," Jack returned. "I'm trying to find a diamond mine near your property. Kandy said you had maps in that safe. I was looking for the maps and I grabbed those folders. I thought they might be it."

"Oh, jeesh." Madison skimmed a hand through her short-cropped hair. "The diamond mine. I forgot about that."

"Diamond mine?" Marley scoffed.

Just for fun, he belted Jack again. Madison began to quiver with anger. She felt like smashing the set. She never had liked that jerk. Sure, he'd hit Jack while Jack was tied down and couldn't defend himself. "I'd like to see him in a fair fight," she muttered.

"Did you seriously think you could fool me with your nonsense about a diamond mine?" Marley asked in a sniveling, snarly voice. "There are no diamond mines in Texas and none anywhere near here, either. I knew it was a ruse the minute that stupid waitress came running to me with it. It was a diversion, to get my attention away from your plan to break into my home. You thought I'd be out digging holes from here to kingdom come, looking for diamonds, and you could just waltz in here and take my notebooks."

"I don't know anything about any notebooks," Jack shot back.

"Where's the other one?" Marley raged. "Where's the other Roderick Tweed notebook?"

"The other...what?" Safe in her lonely surveillance room, Madison sat up straighter. She had the notebook in question. But what did it have to do with Roderick Tweed?

This was getting crazier and more complicated by the minute. If Madison was following Marley's rantings and ravings properly, then there were no diamond mines, only notebooks. And Roderick Tweed notebooks, to boot.

"I don't understand," she said out loud.

Dazed, Madison picked up the heavy leather binder from where she'd dropped it after she'd beaned the guard. Slowly, she opened the front cover and then, in the same numb fashion, began to inspect its contents.

"It's one of Tweed's bibles," she murmured, not believing what she was seeing. Flipping pages more quickly, she knew what it was, but it didn't seem possible. Why here? She'd seen its like before, years ago, back when she was a hack who wrote for Roderick Tweed.

Each time he came up with an idea for a new book, old Mr. Tweed would develop the bible himself, including copious notes, a complete outline and sketches of all his research, upon which the actual writer would base the book once it was assigned.

But the writers only got bits and pieces of it at a time, maybe enough for a chapter today and a scene tomorrow. It was a security precaution, so that nobody could steal Roderick Tweed's ideas or write the books themselves. Security on these "bibles" was supertight, and everybody knew that they were worth their weight in gold.

"If this is the bible for the new Roderick Tweed book and Marley stole it, it's worth millions," she whispered. Who needed diamonds when a guaranteed billion seller was sitting in your lap? "He could write the book himself, or maybe...maybe just destroy it."

After all, they'd said time and time again that they despised Roderick Tweed for keeping them slaves all those years. They'd even plotted revenge in their spare hours.

"But that was just a joke!" Madison argued. Wasn't it?

Now that she thought about it, she recalled that Marley had been the most vocal of anyone in his animosity toward the Big Author Upstairs. And Marley had never struck her as all that rational or stable, either, if she was telling the complete truth.

"Maybe he fell over the edge," Madison mused. "Maybe he went bonkers, insane, bananas. He'd have to be nuts to treat Jack this way. So maybe he doesn't want to write the book. Maybe he doesn't want anyone to write it."

But the biggest question remained. "What the hell does this have to do with Jack?"

"Tweed sent you, didn't he?" Marley asked, grilling Jack unmercifully. "He hired you to steal the notebooks, didn't he?"

"You stole them, Carlos. Getting 'em back is justice, not theft."

"Don't talk to me like that!" Marley was fit to be tied, jumping from foot to foot, waving the gun in the air, acting like a maniac.

Madison was frightened, even if Jack wasn't. "Don't bait him, you idiot," she yelled at the screen. "Tell him the truth!"

But her mind was a muddle. What was the truth? There was no earthly reason for Jack to be breaking into haciendas and endangering both of them, all for Roderick Tweed. Or at least, no reason that she knew of.

Unfortunately, she now realized she knew very little about Jack. She'd never been able to verify the slightest detail about him, and he'd certainly never offered any useful information.

When push came to shove, she knew how he made love, she knew what the curve of his hip looked like and how the hair on his chest tapered down to his...

She swallowed. Even here, even now, he had the power to reach out and shock her, to make her melt into a puddle of desire. *But who was he?*

When she'd met him, she'd decided he was a private investigator. And then when she'd found out about the diamond mine, she'd changed her mind, deciding he was a thief.

It now appeared that the diamond mine was all a scam, just to get him inside Marley's place. So he'd planned to steal the notebooks all along, and it was only after they were shot at that he'd sped up his timetable.

So far, so good. That all made sense.

Her head was pounding and she was dizzy enough to throw up, if she wasn't careful. Did anything make sense? Was she really on to something here?

"No diamonds, no thief," she said out loud. Jack was not a thief. So did that mean she should go back to choice number one?

"Tweed hired you, didn't he?" Marley shouted, punctuating her thoughts.

So was Jack really a private eye, hired by old Tweed himself? Madison spun around in the guard's chair, trying to come to grips with any of this. She did remember he'd said he'd heard of Tweed back there at the beginning. But why wouldn't he have told her if he was working for Roderick Tweed? Why keep it such a big secret?

"Tell me," Marley practically shrieked, grabbing Jack's collar and choking at him. "Who are you to Roderick Tweed?"

And then it hit her. Like a ton of bricks, it slammed into the forefront of her brain.

"It's not who he is to Roderick Tweed," she whispered, staring at the screen. "He *is* Roderick Tweed. Jack is Roderick Tweed."

Chapter Thirteen

Black Jack sniffed the air suspiciously. Smoke. And where there was smoke, there was fire.

"Holy hell," he said out loud. Nell had set the place on fire! He'd needed a diversion, but he hadn't asked for all-out devastation. "Nell, where are you?" he yelled, peering through the murky air. But there was no sight of her. Quickly, he rushed down the red velvet stairs and out onto the street.

But it was too late. The Pleasure Palace Dance Hall and Gambling Establishment was nothing but ashes.

She'd saved his hide yet again. And he was going to kill her if he ever got his hands on her.

Black Jack Brogan, Book #4
Hit the Jack Pot

Agitated, Madison stood and paced in front of the monitors. She was stunned. "Jack is Roderick Tweed," she said again, but it was no more believable this time.

"No, he can't be," she said firmly. "He cannot be."

Everybody knew that Roderick Tweed was an ancient fuddy-duddy—feeble, strange, and reclusive. A downright oddball. How did that translate to Jack? Jack was none of those things.

"But nobody really knows how old Tweed is," she reminded herself. "There were rumors, but nobody ever saw him. All those years, he could've been a dead ringer for Abraham Lincoln, or Tom Cruise, for that matter. Nobody ever saw him."

And as for the rest of the Roderick Tweed traits, well, nobody really knew about them, either, when it came right down to it. Since there was no one to contradict the theories, people could make up anything they wanted to.

If Jack really was Roderick Tweed, he might even have encouraged the strange rumors, to maintain his anonymity, to allow him to travel anywhere he wanted to while trying out his famous field-research techniques. Roderick Tweed was a celebrity, and his multitude of fans might have driven him crazy. But if nobody knew who he was or what he looked like, he was free to come and go as he pleased, to research to his heart's content.

And once he'd done the research himself, once he'd plotted his huge global sagas, he was free to farm the real work out to hacks like young Madison Talley, to rob them of their work and not give them credit.

"Oh, Jack..." she moaned. "How can you be Roderick Tweed?"

She searched his fuzzy image on the screen, but it didn't provide any answers.

In certain ways, it made such perfect sense. There were the notebooks, first of all. If there were no diamond mines—and Marley had made that much clear—then she had to conclude that Jack had set up shop in Godforsaken just to get the notebooks back. And why would he do that?

Only one reason she could think of. Because they were his.

"It fits," she muttered.

When they found out that Kandy was faxing Jack's things to Carlos, what happened? Jack was furious, all out of proportion to Kandy's annoying, but not terribly damaging crime. Madison had thought at the time that Jack's reaction seemed very harsh and very personal.

This has gone on too long, he'd said, when she'd questioned him. *We get back what's mine and we do it now.*

"He said he was going to get back what was his." She fingered the leather binder. "And what was his was these damn notebooks."

Now that she thought about it, a few other tidbits fell into place. Like Jack's presence at the Literary Ball. Hadn't there been a rumor that Roderick Tweed was expected? And who'd arrived? Jack.

At the time it hadn't occurred to her to wonder how he'd gotten into an invitation-only party. But now she knew. If he was Roderick Tweed, he was invited.

"And then there was my invitation," she said slowly. Those circumstances had been unusual, too.

She hadn't expected to be asked in the first place, and when she had it had been weeks after everyone else.

Her very tardy invitation had come through her agent, Harvey Thornton, who just happened to also be the agent of Roderick Tweed. Jack had positively jumped when she'd mentioned Harvey's name the first time, as if he'd recognized it. Of course he recognized it—Harvey was his agent, too!

She could imagine it all so clearly: she had been bothering Jack, threatening to tag along on whatever he did, so he'd simply called up their mutual agent and secured her an invitation. Why? To get her out of town.

If it wasn't a conspiracy, why would she have been invited at the last possible minute? Why would he have shown up, too? And why would he have a vested interest in the damn notebooks?

There was one more factor to consider. Her manuscript of *Between a Jack and a Hard Place,* the one he'd read and quoted from, even though the book wasn't published yet.

I have connections, he'd said. And what connection, other than that double-dealing skunk, Harvey, would've given him a copy of her manuscript?

"Jack, you cad," she accused the television monitor. "I could kill you right now." Instead, she was going to have to save him. "And then I'll kill you," she promised his image on the screen.

A healthy dose of fury had cleared her mind, made her ready to do battle. She knew what she had to do, and she had to get rid of the guard in the closet for starters.

With adrenaline and anger pounding in her veins, she got a good grip on the gun and then jerked open the closet door, already pointing her pistol. But the guard was still completely out of it. Swearing a blue streak, Madison dragged him out and with much effort got him half dangled over the seat of the chair, which fortunately rolled on casters. Once he was on the chair, it was a fairly easy matter to wheel the guard out into the next room. With a flourish, Madison locked him out there in the anteroom.

With the guard out of the way, she went back into the surveillance room. Marley and Jack were still fighting down in the library, but not for long, she vowed. Humming to herself, she bent over and started switching alarms. She flipped one button after the other, from the kitchen-window alarm to the one on the terrace, from the front gate to the four separate alarms wired to the twelve-car garage. When she was done, the whole house shook with the combined wails and shrieks of about fifty different alarms, emanating from and broadcast to every room in the house.

"That ought to keep everybody hopping," she said with satisfaction. By the time the security forces traced all those conflicting signals, they'd be worn out. Just to be sure, she flipped on all the intercoms and ordered, "Red alert. All forces to the rose garden. Everyone, report at once to the rose garden."

Now she hoped there *was* a rose garden.

Her own intercom buzzed and she stepped back. On the library monitor, Marley spoke impatiently into a box near the door.

"This is Carlos," he snapped over the intercom. "What's going on up there? We better be under attack from the marines to explain all those damn alarms."

She took a deep breath. It was now or never. Dropping her voice as low as it would go, she pushed the intercom button and growled, "It's not the marines, but you're gonna wish it was. The surveillance room, the alarm system and the intercom are now under my control. I have you on camera, so don't try anything funny."

"Who are you?" Marley cried, peering up into the corner of the room that held the camera.

Even on the grainy black-and-white TV, Madison could see Jack's face clearly in the background of her picture. When her voice sounded in the room, a look of dark anger crossed his face, drawing his black brows together, as if he was furious at her for not running like hell and leaving him to fend for himself.

But then he shook his head, as if he should've known better. A glimmer of a smile curved his lips and he struggled against his bonds so he could face the TV camera at a better angle. "Mad," he mouthed, "I love you."

Her heart melted and she blew a kiss at him. Lying, thieving, cheating hound dog that he was, she still loved him with every nerve ending in her body.

"Who are you?" Marley demanded. "What do you want?"

She had no intention of telling Marley her name, although it would've been fun to see his jaw drop down to his drawers. But she wanted all the knowledge on her side and all the uncertainty on his. To that end, she had to remind herself to keep calling him Carlos. Any slip, and he'd know she was connected to his real life. This way, he was in the dark.

"Your security forces are scattered all over, answering all the alarms I set off," she told him coolly. She reached over, into the Locks column, and knocked back the tab marked Library. The responding clicks were audible over the intercom and the television monitor, in stereo. "I've just locked you into the library, so you can't move, Carlos. You're stuck like a rat on a sinking ship."

"What do you want?" he called out, looking completely unconcerned.

"Drop your gun and then untie my partner," she commanded.

"No way!"

After moving the knob on her side of the intercom all the way up to the maximum volume, she took the guard's gun between both hands and bravely pointed it at the monitor showing the kitchen. She turned her head, squeezed her eyes shut and then wrenched the trigger. Ka-boom!

It was louder and scarier than she'd expected, and she reeled backward from the recoil. Meanwhile, there was a huge, jagged hole in the front of the television, with wires and sparks buzzing at her.

"Did you hear that?" she demanded. "I blew a hole in a TV, and I'll keep doing it until you let my partner go."

"What do I care if you vandalize my televisions?" Marley said with a snide laugh.

Good point. Think, Madison, think. What would get to Marley?

She knew the man; she'd worked with the man for three years. She had to know something she could use against him.

She quickly considered and rejected the idea of running down there and pointing her gun at him. For one thing she had no route to get there, and for another Marley had always boasted of being an expert marksman. Once he saw who it was on the other end of the gun, he'd laugh in her face.

No, there had to be a better choice than that. "What does Marley really hate?" she mumbled. "What?"

Snakes, spiders, rats, heights—none of the usual things rang any bells. And then it hit her.

"Fire," she said slowly. Once when they'd had a writers' meeting somebody's cigarette hit a paper wad and started a small blaze in the ashtray, and Marley had run screaming out of the room. Fire was the answer.

"It's not the TVs you should worry about. I'm starting fires up here, Carlos," she declared into the intercom. She blasted another set, just for the satisfaction of watching Marley's face when the horrible boom sounded.

She waited eagerly for flames. Unfortunately, there was nothing more than a few measly sparks. Apparently, blowing up TV sets wasn't the best way to get a good blaze going. Hopefully, Marley didn't know that, however.

"Fires? What do you mean?"

"As big a bonfire as I can make. And I've got a lot of electrical equipment to play with, plus the cigarette lighter your guard so thoughtfully left behind when he finished with his nasty cigar." She held up the lighter, ticking the flame on and off. What kind of damage could she do with that?

"You're bluffing," Marley shouted.

With a frown, she flicked on the lighter and set it over by the wires on the blasted TV. The smell of burning plastic filled the air. For good measure, she tossed some loose papers into a flimsy wastebasket and set that on fire, too. By hook or by crook, she was determined to start a conflagration of epic proportions.

Into the intercom, she announced, "There should be some really neat fireworks by the time I get done."

She smiled. She was starting to enjoy this new, nasty side of her personality.

"Don't worry about me, though," she called out loudly. "I'll have plenty of time to get out alive." She leaned in very close to the speaker so her voice would boom out at him. "But you're locked in the library. It might take hours to get you out, hours of smoke inhalation and big, bad flames licking at your fat little rump. You'll be a dead, roasted rat, Carlos."

"You won't burn up your partner," he insisted.

"You're right," she improvised. "I won't. No, I'll come and rescue him. It's just you I'll leave trapped in the Towering Inferno. Want to try me?"

"You're on the third floor," he blustered, but he was clearly getting nervous, waving his gun more haphazardly, beginning to perspire. "I'm way over on the other side of the first floor. How will your silly fire get to me?"

As if to punctuate her words, the flames in the wastebasket really started to heat up, beginning to melt the plastic of the basket itself and setting off the smoke alarm over her head.

"Can you hear that?" she shouted. "Smoke alarm number one. Want to see how fast my fire spreads?"

The portly man began to sweat so profusely that even on the monitor, she could see the rivulets running down the sides of his face. "N-no," he stuttered. "I'll do what you want."

"Drop your gun. Now!" she said sharply. "And then untie him."

"Look," he said, throwing up his hands as he ran over to Jack. "I'm letting him go, see?"

"Good. Don't forget the gun." She waited a few moments, until she was sure Jack was free and had Marley's gun in his possession. Finally, he stood up and gave her the okay sign and she breathed a definite sigh of relief. "Jack, tie him up!" she shouted, but he'd beaten her to it, and already had Marley in the chair and lashed down before the words were out of her mouth.

"Unlock the doors," he shouted, and she complied.

"Jack, the fire is getting worse up here," she coughed, as smoke began to billow out of the wastebasket. "Where should I meet you?"

"Front door?"

"How do I get there?"

"You mean you don't know?"

"No, I don't know!" she cried. "If I'd known, I would've rescued you and gotten out of here a long time ago."

"Didn't you look at the maps when I told you to?"

"I don't read maps very well, okay? I'm an idiot, all right?" she said angrily. "But I'm still the idiot who saved your bacon, buddy boy!"

"Be quiet, will you? Stay where you are," he shouted back, already racing for the door of the library, carrying Marley's gun in one hand and the notebooks that had caused so much trouble under the other arm. "I'll get you."

"Oh, hellfire," she muttered.

That's exactly what it felt like in this smoke-filled room, where the flames were licking up the walls from the melted wastebasket and heat was beginning to radiate from everywhere around her.

Picking up her own notebook, Madison dashed out into the anteroom, where the guard was still lying prone over the chair. Rolling him along, she opened the door and trundled out into the hallway, where she waited anxiously for Jack. Who'd get there first, him or the flames from the room behind her?

As the seconds dragged on, Madison's anxiety level rose and rose. Where was he? How long could she last?

It seemed like it took forever, but finally there he was, rounding the corner at one end of the long hall.

"Thank God," she exclaimed. She threw herself at him with all the energy she had left. "I've never been so happy to see anyone in my entire life." But she drew back. "I don't know whether to kiss you, because I'm so relieved you're alive, or to beat the hell out of you."

She decided a good slap would be a lot more satisfying. When her palm connected with his infuriating cheek, creating a resounding *smack,* she knew she'd made the right choice.

"What was that for?"

"Roderick Tweed," she said hotly.

"Can we discuss this later? The house is burning down," he reminded her.

"All right. But don't think this is the end of it."

He sighed. "With you, there's never an end to it." And then it was his turn to jump back. "What's this?" he asked in disbelief, pointing at the man on the chair, partially hidden by the notebook she'd laid on top of him.

"Well, I could hardly leave him." Madison pushed the chair ahead of her as she hurried back in the direction Jack had come from. "I just want to dump him somewhere safe."

"You're torching the house and you're concerned about the guards you may burn up in the process?"

"Of course!" She kept on pushing the chair, until Jack grabbed her arm to stop her.

"This way," he said, taking a different corridor. "If you're going to have wheels with you, we'll have to take the elevator."

"Elevator? But elevators aren't safe in fires."

"Nothing's safe in a fire, Mad," he said dryly, as he hauled her and her comatose guard into the small elevator.

Thankfully, the ride was very short. As the doors slid open, they bolted out onto the first floor and then took a straight path out of the hacienda. Thank goodness Jack seemed to have no trouble with the mansion's twists and turns. Once they had cleared the door, Madison rolled her guard over to a spot on the terrace and retrieved the notebook. Then she and Jack took off.

Behind them, orange flames flickered from several upstairs windows and guards began running around, trying to get people out and get hoses going. To her relief, Madison saw both the old woman who'd been dozing and Marley himself jumping up and down and shouting outside the hacienda, so they'd obviously escaped in plenty of time.

But she didn't have time to worry about the occupants of Marley's hacienda. As the blaze burned hotter and the flames grew higher, raging against the darkness, Jack took all of the notebooks. He began to run.

It was way past time to get away from here, to get back across the border into Texas, before anybody spotted them or followed them. Madison scurried to keep up with him.

"The car," he shouted. "Come on, Mad. Run!"

She had no breath left and a terrible stitch in her side by the time they finally got to the place where they'd stashed their getaway car. Madison had never been so thrilled to see a '73 Ford Pinto. Gasping for air, she collapsed into her seat. She barely had the door shut when the engine revved to life and Jack steered them away from the whole sorry episode of Carlos's hacienda.

"Jack," she said, trying to sit up, "you're smiling. What in God's name is wrong with you?"

His teeth flashed white in that handsome face. "We've got the notebooks. Mission completed, Mad. And successfully."

"You call that successfully?" She felt her mouth drop open. "We burned a place to the ground. We created an enemy for life. And all for a bunch of stupid notebooks!"

"These aren't stupid." The line of his jaw was firm, brooking no disagreement. "A lot of people's lives depended on me getting these back."

"Give me a break!" she shouted. "Your livelihood, that's all."

"What's that supposed to mean?"

"The Roderick Tweed notebooks," she snapped. "I looked at the one I had. Of course I knew what it was.

Did you forget I used to work for him? Or should I say, work for you?"

"Me?" he asked warily.

"You," she said more emphatically. "Roderick Tweed." She remembered the first time she'd told him her name, and he'd said snidely, *What do they call you for short? Mad?* Well, turnabout was fair play. "So tell me, Roderick," she said mockingly. "What do they call you for short? Ick?"

There was a long pause. "You have this all wrong," he said finally.

But she cut him off. "Oh, baloney. It all makes sense." She ran a hand through her hair. "The invitation to the ball...you getting in...you knowing Harvey... Not to mention the fact that the notebooks are so damned important to you."

"Yes, the notebooks are important, but not for the reason you think. If you'll let me—"

"And why should I? Why should I believe anything you say?" she demanded. "You've lied to me from the very beginning—all that junk about runaways and diamond mines and private eyes. You wouldn't know a private eye if you fell over one!"

"Obviously, neither would you," he muttered.

"I never lied to you," she said softly. "Never."

"I know." He sighed again. "Madison, I had no choice. I had to keep you in the dark. If you'll just let me explain—"

"No," she interrupted. She crossed her arms over that damn, hot turtleneck. "If I let you talk, you'll just manufacture more lies to keep me happy. I know

now, Jack, so we both might as well face it. You're Roderick Tweed, and I hate your guts. I fell in love with you and I hate you. I always have. I wrote your damn books, you jerk!" She reached over and hit him on the shoulder, relishing it when he winced. "You cad, you slimeball, you thief!" she spat out, punching him with every epithet.

"Madison—"

But there was no holding her back once she was on a roll. Madison had no intention of sitting still and letting him convince her once again that the sky was red, that the moon was made of green cheese, that pigs could fly and women without a good grip on reality could fall in love and not end up with their hearts broken.

So she called him every name in the book, using every swear word she'd heard in that horrible cantina in Godforsaken, and even making up a few on the spur of the moment. All he could do was cast bitter, frustrated glances her way, until he suddenly pulled the car to a stop and turned off the ignition.

"Why are you stopping?" she asked. "We're not in Laredo."

"Change of plans," he said tersely. He got out and took the notebooks with him.

"Change of plans?" Like walking all the way to Laredo? But when she opened her door, she saw that Jack was hiking toward a small plane. "That's the same plane," she said in surprise. "The plane we flew from Seattle in. What's it doing here?"

"It's flying us over the border."

"But you told me..." Madison glared at him. "Another deception, Jack? You tell me we're going through Laredo by car, and then you steal another plane?"

"In the first place, it's not stolen," he said grimly, with his jaw clenched so tightly she couldn't figure out how he could get words out. "In the second place, I didn't tell you because I didn't see that it made a whole lot of difference."

But Madison was still hurting, and she didn't heed the warning signs. "And I suppose all the other things you lied to me about didn't make any difference, either, huh?"

"Damn it, Madison, I've had about as much as I can take," he said violently. "I've been tied up, beat up and laughed at by a crazy man, and then rescued by the woman I love, when *I'm* the one who's supposed to be doing the rescuing, damn it!"

As she stood there, shocked down to the ground by his outburst, he grabbed her arm, hauled her into his arms and hoisted her over his shoulder.

"What do you think you're doing?" she tried to ask, but her words were bouncing off his back.

"I'm taking you onto my plane and I'm getting us the hell out of here," he growled.

"But—"

"No buts. I only know one way to keep you quiet, Madison, and that's to make love to you." Fiercely, he added, "And I plan to do it all night, if necessary."

Chapter Fourteen

New Orleans was hotter than blazes, with air so still and heavy he could feel it wrap around him, choking his life away. Black Jack narrowed his steely gaze at the soiled doves beckoning so seductively from their porches.

Their luscious charms were not for him. Not this time.

He had an appointment with a lady, a lady with something he wanted and wanted bad.

Desirée DuBois, with her voodoo spells and her dark Creole beauty, was about as much woman as he could handle.

Desirée wanted him. Love potions and amulets, trips to Madame Giselle, little dolls made in his image with hanks of his hair.... Yes, Desirée wanted him.

She wanted his secrets. She wanted his soul.

Black Jack Brogan, Book # 11
Jack Magic

Jack swept her up into the plane and tossed her down on the bed.

"Bed?" Madison sat up and looked around. It was the same plane, all right, but now it had a bed attached to the back wall instead of a love seat. The side seats were gone, too, replaced by a television set and VCR on one side and a sort of dry sink/portable-butler thing opposite, currently holding a silver ice bucket and a bottle of champagne. "Jack?" she asked doubtfully. "What is all this?"

"The hands-off policy is officially over," he said meaningfully, advancing on her. "I arranged a small celebration."

"You're kidding. For me?"

That stopped him in his tracks. "Who the hell do you think it's for?"

"I don't know." She glanced around, still not quite understanding. This was so romantic, so sweet, so... unlike Jack. "I find it hard to believe that you had time to set all this up in between studying maps and finding out about Marley's security systems."

"Marley? His name was Carlos."

"I'll tell you about it later," she said impatiently, not willing to go into that at such a critical and confusing moment.

As she watched, Jack shoved closed the outside door on the tiny plane, trapping them in here, together. Alone. All she could think about was the last time they'd been on this plane and what they'd done... on the floor.

Madison took a deep breath. It was not going to happen again. She was going to keep fighting with Jack, skewering him, until they were both sure that they didn't belong together.

"So what about all this stuff?" she prompted, waving a hand at the champagne bucket. "Why did you do it?"

A long pause hung between them.

"Why?" she asked again.

"Because I love you." Jack stood very still, watching her from under those dark, slanting brows. "I did it because I love you."

"Oh." He was good. Her resolve began to weaken and melt away.

"I love you," he repeated, louder this time, as if the idea was getting clearer the more times he said it.

Madison cowered on the bed, not sure how to react, but Jack just kept staring at her, with a gaze that grew warmer and more assured by the second. It only took him two quick strides to get to the bed. And then he was there, next to her, holding her fast in the hard circle of his arms.

"Ahem," someone said from the front of the plane.

Startled, they both looked up.

"You folks ready to take off?" the pilot asked sheepishly, poking his head around the door into the cockpit.

"Ready," Jack said curtly. Madison didn't say anything at all. She was too busy swooning.

As the pilot disappeared, Jack leapt up and locked the door. "No more interruptions," he promised, and then he jumped back in beside her. He was nibbling her ears, biting her and kissing her, giving her such a rush of warmth and desire that she moaned and slid back into the bedclothes.

"I told myself I wouldn't fall for this again," she said with a little wail of distress. "But, Jack, you're so good at this. To think that Roderick Tweed would turn out like this."

"For the last time, Madison, I'm not Roderick Tweed."

And then his hot, demanding mouth covered hers, devouring her, meeting her head-on with a passion so direct and so overpowering she couldn't have resisted if she'd wanted to.

She didn't. She wanted more. Lots more.

She helped him strip off her turtleneck and his, greedily pushing the fabric aside.

"Madison," he said unevenly, when her bare, pale skin was revealed to his eyes. "You weren't wearing anything under your shirt?"

"Oh, well," she said bravely, suddenly feeling very naked and very small under his rapt gaze. "It was black and it was so hot, and I'm not very big in that, um, area, so it wasn't like I needed a bra or anything—"

But he stopped her with a hard kiss. "You're perfect," he said roughly, cupping her small breasts, teasing the nipples with his thumbs, driving her absolutely stark raving mad so quickly she couldn't believe it. She held on to his strong, muscled back, stroking and massaging him, brushing kisses all over his dark, softly whiskered jaw and across his lips, trying to find again that deep kiss that made her feel so good.

And the plane began to climb.

It rumbled underneath them, jiggling them, knocking them together and apart ever so slightly, pressing her thigh into the front of his jeans, brushing her breast across his chest, lending an unsteady, tantalizing rhythm to every touch, every kiss, every caress.

"Madison," he growled, low in his throat. "Quit wiggling. You're making me wild."

"It's not me, it's turbulence," she tried to tell him, but even she wasn't sure. Falling backward onto the bed, she slipped her hands to his face, pulling him to her mouth with all the strength she could muster, tasting his tongue, exulting in his savage kiss.

Still pressed into the breath-defying kiss, she rolled over on top of him, setting a hand on the top button of his black jeans, popping it open without remorse. That small noise was all it took to stoke the fires even higher, until they were both slashing buttons and throwing the rest of their clothes to the four winds.

And then there they were, naked and slick with desire, laughing and gasping for breath as they wound into the cool sheets of the plane's small bed. The jet continued to buck and jump under them, adding a dimension of unpredictability to the proceedings, but it only made things more exciting.

All Madison knew was that she was on fire, that Jack's hands and mouth were everywhere, until it felt like flames were licking her from the inside out. She spiraled from one height to the next, holding him, feeling him around her. She tried hard to take her time, to look and touch her fill, as she investigated the hard landscape of Jack's beautiful body. She loved the lean sinew of his flanks, where waist tapered into hips, the taut, corded perfection of his arms and his chest and the soft, sleek feel of the hair at his neck as it drifted through her fingers. He was the most gorgeous man she'd ever seen, ever imagined, and he was hers. At least for this moment.

After their long night of fire and recrimination, she was exhausted. And yet she kept finding stores of energy she didn't know she had, arching against him, running her hands over him, loving him. She had never been so caught up in something so fierce, so unforgiving and so incredibly erotic.

She reached for him, trying to guide him inside, but he resisted, still toying with her, stroking her, back and forth, as slow as molasses, as insubstantial as a feather. He hovered there, just out of reach, driving her absolutely insane on purpose. Somewhere in the recesses of her conscious mind, she feared she was going to start screaming.

The plane took a dip, Jack bumped against her more fully than he'd planned, and there it was—the touch that turned the tide. She was dying, flaming, moaning out loud, as waves of heat swept over her like brushfire.

"Jack," she cried, locking him in her arms, practically squeezing the life out of him. And then she spun over, on top, sliding onto him. His hands rode her hips hard as she positioned herself and took him inside.

She tried to set the pace, to make it languorous and deep and unbearably slow, but he cheated. With a muttered oath, Jack pulled her back underneath him. Bracing himself on his arms, he stroked smoothly, quickly, sighing with pure pleasure and whispering her name. She felt her skin flush and tingle as her desire mounted yet again.

"Madison," he said, going rigid.

"Oh, yes," she breathed.

And then the plane hit a huge air pocket.

"Oh, no!" Madison shouted, as they fell off the bed and onto the floor, still hopelessly entwined.

Jack was laughing and moaning as he held her against his chest. Helplessly, he muttered, "I think I have bruises on every inch of my body."

"Oh, Jack..." was the best Madison could do. Tangled across him, still warm from his embrace, she felt faint from effort, worn out from experiencing so many feelings and so much pleasure, all smashed together into one incredible, dizzy, electrifying episode.

"Come on," he said gently. Rising, he swept her into his arms and tucked her back into the bed.

When he slipped in beside her, she snuggled in closer and let her eyelids drift shut. A nap spent securely in Jack's arms sounded better than anything she could imagine.

"Jack?" she murmured drowsily. "Wake me up before we land. I want time to put some clothes on this time."

"We're not landing," he told her, dropping soft kisses on her forehead and the tip of her nose.

"Not landing?" She opened one eye. "How can we not land?"

"I told the pilot to keep going until I'm ready to come down."

Leaning back against his shoulder, she gave him a smile. "Are you ready yet?"

"No," he said clearly. "Not by a long shot."

THEY FLEW THROUGH the night, stopping briefly to refuel and then setting off again.

By the time they were nearing Alaska, Madison was sipping champagne from a crystal flute and feeling very mellow indeed. Jack had even packed a wardrobe for each of them, so she relaxed in a big T-shirt and shorts and Jack pulled on jeans and a black denim shirt as he padded over to put *Gunga Din* in the VCR.

She felt like it was a cozy date at home, as they sat comfortably in the bed and watched the black-and-white images flicker across the screen. All they needed was popcorn.

"So thoughtful of you to remember the cookies," she murmured, munching her way through a box. It wasn't popcorn, but it would do.

"I know you too well to forget the food," he replied.

"Aren't you sweet?" After a brief pause to kiss him properly, Madison turned back to the question that had been bothering her. "So tell me." She waved a hand at the television. "Why *Gunga Din*?"

"I like it," he said simply.

"I suppose that's good enough," she said doubtfully. "Although I have to say, it seems to hold more significance to you than that."

"There is one more thing."

"Well? What is it?"

"My real name..."

"Is Roderick Tweed," she finished for him. Positioning a pillow behind her, she sat back and gave him a reproving look. "We already settled that, Jack. I mean, you'll always be Jack to me, but the Tweed jig is up. I know who you are and I don't care." She paused. "Well, I care, but I'm willing to overlook it."

Quickly he covered her lips with his, kissing her until she was breathless. "You don't understand, Madison," he said slowly, still holding her firmly by the shoulders. "I have to tell you something that I swore I'd never reveal."

"Let's not play cops-and-robbers here, Jack." But the severity of his expression was starting to scare her. Could this new story possibly be true? "Just tell me," she ordered.

"Will you promise never to breathe a word of this? Ever."

"Of course." Next he was going to be asking her to sign in blood. But at his dark look, she added, "I promise, Jack. I swear. Cross my heart and hope to die."

"Oh, God. I'm crazy to tell you this," he muttered.

"You don't have a choice," she said sweetly. "I'm never going to give up until I know. And you know how diligent I can be when I want something."

"Lola," he said gloomily.

"Lola?" She flushed faintly. "I keep forgetting you've read all of those. Well, not exactly like Lola. At the moment, Jack, you don't have any clothes to snip off, even if I wanted to." She sent him a hungry glance. "And there was a time when I really wanted to."

"Madison," he said gruffly, "we're never going to get through this unless you behave yourself."

She took a deep, cleansing breath and sat patiently on her side of the bed. "I'm behaving myself. So get on with it, will you?"

"I'm not Roderick Tweed."

"Mmm-hmm." She waited. "And . . . ?"

"There isn't one."

"There isn't one what?"

"Roderick Tweed," he said flatly. "There is no Roderick Tweed."

"I don't understand."

"There is no Roderick Tweed," he said again.

"No Roderick Tweed?" She scooted closer, trying gamely to figure out this new wrinkle. "But what about the books? Who wrote the books?"

"Madison, you wrote the books," Jack returned. "You ought to know that."

"No, I don't mean who did the actual writing. I mean, who made all those outlines and the indexes and the character sketches?" She crossed her arms over her chest implacably. "There was somebody creating those Tweed bibles, somebody back there pulling those strings."

"Me." Jack slumped back into the pillows. "Harvey Thornton, me, and three other men. We created Roderick Tweed."

"But why?"

"As a cover." Reaching over her, Jack took her champagne glass and knocked back a healthy swallow. "We were a small, very secret cadre, doing intelligence work for the government."

Madison hesitated. "This is a joke, right?"

"It's no joke." He ran a hand through his hair. "Good grief, Mad, I tell you lies for weeks and you believe every word. I finally get around to the truth and *now* you choose not to believe me."

"So you're saying you're a spy?" she asked carefully.

Well, this was a novel approach, she'd give him that. Jack, a spy. Damn him, if it didn't ring true. And damn him, if it wasn't even more exciting, more dangerous and more seductive than being a private eye or a thief.

A spy. Oh, dear. She was in trouble.

Trust Jack to trump her fantasies.

"I *was* a spy," he corrected her. "I retired."

"Oh, well, thank heaven for small favors."

"What?"

"Nothing." She shook her head. Jack as a retired spy was only slightly better than Jack as a spy, but she was grateful for the respite from her heated, heavenly thoughts, nonetheless. Goodness gracious, the books she could write when this was all over. She had enough stories to scorch her readers' fingers as they turned the pages.

"Okay." Still looking grim, he continued on his Roderick Tweed tale. "We needed to get into a lot of dangerous places, with no questions asked. It was pretty much of a joke at first, something Harvey got us going on once when we were all drunk as skunks and trading anecdotes."

"Wait a minute." Her head was spinning. "Are you saying Roderick Tweed was an accident? And Harvey is a spy, too? Those books were billion sellers. And they were an accident?"

"Harvey was our contact. He never did fieldwork. But yes, the books were an accident. We made up the outline for the first one based on incidents from our real assignments that we strung together." Jack raised his beautiful shoulders in an expressive shrug. "We were as surprised as anybody when the books took off. But that's what made the cover work. Once we had Tweed to hide behind, we could go anywhere. We got a lot done under the guise of Tweed's field research. Roderick Tweed wrote books set all over the map."

"The perfect cover...."

"Exactly." He shifted in the bed, meeting her gaze more directly. "And that's why the notebooks were so important. Not just to me, but to all of us. If anybody looked closely, they'd know the truth."

"But how?"

"Those were the originals, not the cleaned-up versions we circulated to the authors," he said moodily. "There were all kinds of notes and messages, code words, whatever. We all sent things in to Harvey to create Tweed books—whatever we had to keep the identity going. It was all in those notebooks. They should've been destroyed. Sometimes," he said, glancing over at her, "Harvey is damned foolish."

"But Marley didn't know what he had," Madison insisted. "I'm sure of that. He just wanted to give Tweed a black eye, or maybe write the book himself."

"Who's Marley?"

"Charles Marley. Also known as Carlos, south of the border. He was at the Literary Ball, Jack, and he was also the man holding you at gunpoint." She explained, "I worked with him, back when I was one of the ghostwriting team. There were a bunch of us, with people coming and going over the years, but Marley and I were both there for a while. He always did hate Tweed. I guess that's why he stole the notebooks."

"I don't really care," Jack said, "as long as you believe me."

Madison chewed her lip. "There is no Tweed. You are not Tweed. And you used to be a spy." She considered. "I guess I can handle that."

"Good." For the first time in a long time, Jack offered her a carefree smile. And his fingers came dancing up her leg, tracing the edge of her shorts.

"There's just one thing," she put in, batting at his hand.

Bending to nuzzle her neck, he asked, "What's that?"

"If you're not Roderick Tweed, then who the hell are you?"

Wearily, Jack dropped his head to her shoulder. "That's where *Gunga Din* comes in."

"Your name's not Gunga Din?" she asked, horrified. Who would do that to a child?

"No, it's Cutter. Just like in the movie. Just like on the ID I was carrying that you saw." He slid down into the bedclothes, pulling her with him. "Unlike the guy in the movie, I do have a first name. It's John. John Cutter."

"John Cutter," she mused, trying it on her tongue. "I like it. Not as good as Black Jack Brogan, but not bad, either."

"You know, I had an aunt who called me Jack when I was a kid. I wouldn't mind..."

"Well, Jack, I think that was pretty much a foregone conclusion." She tangled her fingers in his hair. "To me, you'll always be Jack."

"So, Madison, tell me," he said softly, as he began to tickle her and sneak his hands into places they shouldn't have been. "Did you lose your writer's block?"

"Mmm-hmm," she purred. "Very nicely, thank you."

"So what's next on the agenda for Black Jack?" He bit her earlobe gently. "I think you should send him someplace cool, get him out of all that hot weather."

"Naaah," she told him. "I'm thinking of killing off Black Jack."

"What?" Jack sat up straight, dropping her. "How can you kill off Black Jack?"

"I was thinking of keeping him all to myself in the future," she said slyly, and he seemed mollified for the moment. She tapped a finger against her mouth. "You see, Jack, I have this great idea for a new series, kind of mystery/adventures, contemporary, with a lot more sex than my old books."

"More sex? Is that possible?" Jack asked, looking a bit ashen.

But Madison was already swimming along in her new fantasy, and she ignored him. "The Mr. and Mrs. Cutter books. What do you think?"

Jack stiffened in the bed. "Is that a proposal, Madison?"

"Would you say yes if it were?"

He sighed. "Don't I get to do anything in this relationship?"

Madison smiled, her best Dennis the Menace grin. As she reached for Jack's buttons, she whispered, "I know exactly what I want you to do."

Epilogue

A chapter in his life was over. Black Jack swore by all that was holy that he'd never work for the government again.

"I'm my own man now," he said softly, puffing his breath into the frigid Alaska air.

"Alas, Black Jack, I fear you've erred in your conclusion." With a smile, Nell pulled him back inside the warmth of the cabin. Wearing only a blanket, she opened its folds and invited him in. "Now, Mr. Brogan, you're all mine."

And for the first time since he'd met her, Black Jack wasn't planning to argue.

Black Jack Brogan, Book # 18
Jack Mate